KINGDOM OF SAND & STARS

BOOK TWO

TEMPEST MINDS

BY
CANDACE OSMOND

Copyright © 2020 Candace Osmond

Published in Canada by Guardian Publishing.

Library and Archives Canada Cataloguing in Publication.

Kingdom of Sand & Stars/ Candace Osmond

(Tempest Minds; paperback)

First Edition, November 2020

The characters, places, and events portrayed in this book are completely fiction and are in no way meant to represent real people or places. The creation of this book is for fictional purposes and not meant to depict true historical accuracy.

For more information, visit the author's website:

www.authorcandaceosmond.com

GUARDIAN Publishing

Cover Work by Majeau Designs
Facebook.com/MajeauDesigns

All rights reserved.
Copyright 2020 Candace Osmond
ISBN-978-1-988159-79-9

DEDICATION

To Jack and Charlie, the two brightest stars in my universe. Whose brilliant and creative minds never cease to amaze me. I'm so proud to be your mother.

ACKNOWLEDGMENTS

A big thanks to my author bestie, JJ King. She's the first eyes on my rough drafts and my biggest cheerleader.

To my kids, Jack and Charlie, who gave me tons of great ideas for the gods and magic in this new series.

And my partner in life, Corey. Thank you for bringing my Andie Godfrey to life on the covers and for supporting me every step of the way.

CHAPTER ONE

"The sun watches what I do, but the moon knows all my secrets." — **J.M. Wonderland**

The utterly insane things we do in the name of love. They're often our own undoing in the end, and most of us carry that weight of regret to our graves. I thought about that as I lay in a heap in a dark corner of a cell. Moonlight carried through the courtyard just outside and cast striped shadows of the metal bars that contained me across the cold stone floor. But as much as I wanted to…

…I couldn't regret the decisions that brought me here.

I loved Silas with everything I had. Every fiber of my being crawled in a weave through my soul and reached out him. Even in death.

Or what I thought was death.

The possibility of a swift exit was out of reach for me now. Horus had prized me for hours. Too many. The sun had long gone down when he finally tired of driving me with question after question.

Who was I?
Where did I come from?
Where are the Star People hiding?
And lastly,
Where was the portal?

Not once did he punch or kick, or even cut me. He had no need to. My broken leg served as the perfect torture device until I blacked out from the pain, time after time. That was hours ago. The slight change in the sky from jet black to a sultry navy told me so. The sun would be up soon.

My tattered clothes clung to my sweaty skin, and I ached to rip the leather patched jeans from my leg, the one that hung from my body at an odd angle. The skin tight with swelling. The bone had broken immediately on impact when Horus dropped me from the sky. A quick, clean break. For that I was grateful, but almost a day had passed since I got here, and I knew my blood raced with infection. I could practically smell it in the air. The slightest movement sent my nerves into a frenzy, making any form of sleep practically impossible. So, I just sat there, in the corner, fighting for every breath as the toxicity spread through my body.

But that wasn't even the worst part.

My slick and trembling hands gripped my thigh in a futile attempt to stifle the spread of infection, more of a peace of mind really, because all I could think about was the pitcher of wine that sat at the other side of the cell. After hours of prying me with questions I refused to answer, he'd left the wine and some bread before disappearing. Leaving me to stare at it from my dark corner, salivating at the promise it beckoned me with.

Just drag yourself over, drink it. It'll make everything better.

But I couldn't. Not only did every single breath cause me pain, but I couldn't drink it. Not now, not after how far I'd come to fight my addiction. To drink that pitcher would mean starting over again. All the withdrawals, the nausea, the pain. But even worse...

That's exactly what he wants me to do. Loosen my tongue.

I couldn't let that happen.

I stared at that jug all night; every passing minute torturous. But that willpower was melting away as I eyed the clay pitcher in the coming sunlight. An orangey purple light now filtered through the air. My parched tongue slipped out and rubbed over my dry, cracked lips. I could die here in this cell. If I didn't give Horus what he wanted, why would he bother keeping me around? With this probable infection, I was a goner in a matter of days, anyway, regardless of what he did with me.

At least I would go out with a belly warm and full. Appease my demons, and all that.

I took a deep breath and let go of my thigh. A rush of blood pulsed upward, and I inched across the floor. A jolt of pain struck me like lightning, forcing a guttural scream to erupt as it pinned me in place.

"God damnit!" I seethed and bit down on the pain.

My stomach rolled, and I heaved with rapid breaths. I grabbed my leg once again and fought through the swarm of dizziness that threatened to take me down. I couldn't pass out. My skin itched at the thought of what Horus might do to me, *to my body*, when I couldn't at least verbally defend myself.

"Good morning," a voice spoke from outside my cell.

The sound caused the hairs on the back of my neck to stand up as an icy shiver rocked through me. I glanced from the corner of my eye as Horus' figure passed right through the metal bars, just like before. Bare chested under the thin ivory colored cape draped over his shoulders. Intricate sandals laced with gold crunched the sandy floor as he took slow steps across it. He carried another pitcher of wine, accompanied by a tray of actual food this time. Horus motioned at the untouched wine from yesterday and raised his brows at me.

"Not thirsty?"

I sneered up at him from the floor. "Not for that."

"What's the matter?" he replied coyly. "Don't like wine?"

A sickening spasm of pain pulsed up from my leg and I stomped down the urge to scream again as I squeezed my thigh. I rocked back and forth, breathing through it. "N-no, I like it *too* much."

I tipped my head up to find him arching a curious brow and immediately regretted my words. A day of Horus prying me for information, and I managed not to say a thing. The topic of alcohol comes up and I let the weakness fog my mind. Sway my judgement.

I squared my jaw. "*What* do you want?"

Horus approached me slowly, his sandaled feet scratching the sandy floor beneath us. He squatted and set down the food by my side. He was so close; I could smell burn of days of sunshine on his skin. Dark waves fell from his head and drooped to his bare shoulders as he pursed his wide lips and I cringed at the nearness of him. It was too much. A long finger slid under my chin and forced my gaze to meet his. Two dark holes that bored into mine, as if he were searching for a way in.

"To pick up where we left off," he said calmly, unblinking. But the tone didn't match the madness in his eyes. He peered at my leg and the corner of his mouth twitched as he wrapped his hand around it and gave a squeeze. My cries filled the cell, filled the courtyard before bouncing back to clang inside my ears. "Now tell me where the portal is!"

I bit down on my tongue to stifle the fresh pain he inflicted, and my mouth filled with a mix of saliva and blood. I gathered it up before spitting it right in his face. "Never!"

Anger flitted over his expression, but it quickly washed away as Horus wiped the spit from his cheek. He chuckled–an unsettling sound that raked my spine–as he pushed himself to his feet and paced the floor anxiously in thought. He was insane. I threw my head back against the wall behind me, unable to hold it up on my own. Every breath was an amazing feat. I'd give anything to sink into a deep coma right about now.

He quickly came to a stop and faced me, the abrupt movement causing my heart to jump, and I watched as he pulled a dagger from a sheath at his side. Slow and purposeful, allowing the sharp sound to crawl over every one of my nerves. He crouched again, closer this time, his haughty breath smearing across my face while he held the thin blade to my neck.

Eyes bulging with impatience, he gritted the words through his teeth, "Let's try a different question then, shall we?" The sharp edge pressed harder, threatening to draw blood. "*How* did you fix my brother?"

I don't know where the blind courage came from. But it festered up from the depths of my gut and I stared him straight in the eye as I slowly leaned forward, into the blade, breaking my skin. He refused to relent. Warm blood dripped down my neck, but I didn't flinch. Didn't break the hold I had on his challenging glare.

"Never," I said pointedly and as even as I could.

The dagger lingered there for a moment, neither of us willing to let go of the stubbornness that held us in place. Finally, Horus shoved at my chest and I slumped against the wall as he bolted to his feet and began pacing again. He returned the knife to his belt. A frustrated growl echoed off the stone walls and he kicked the plate of food at me; bread and some kind of meat sprinkled the floor.

"Why must you be so...*difficult?*" the unhinged god grumbled loudly, his dark eyes bulging with an otherworldly impatience.

I watched in fear from my corner, waited until he worked through the rage that possessed him. Finally, he cast his face upward and closed his eyes as a deep breath expanded his chest. He held it in for a while before slowly exhaling and chuckled quietly. Confusion pinched my face.

What was so funny?

Horus craned his neck and stared in my direction with a calculating expression that unnerved me to no end. I followed his gaze to the pitcher of wine on the floor and then to the new one he'd brought. My heart sped up, my eyes unblinking while the God of Vengeance bent down to fetch the other jug and placed them both within my reach.

He stood and backed away, a glimmer of mischief in his eye that only grew in response to the fear in mine. He rubbed his hands together before passing through the bars of the cell and disappearing into the shadows of his palace. Leaving me there with my cruel vice wafting promises up to my nose.

"No!" I called out into the dim courtyard. "Take them, *please*!"

A distant laugh carried through the air, and I cried. Hot tears cut through the layers of dirt and dust caked to my cheeks. And I couldn't stop them. I cried for myself, for every inch of sobriety that would inevitably be thrown out the window. Because I knew I wasn't strong enough to resist it. I could quiver behind the excuse of a broken leg all night. But there was nothing in the way of me and those two jugs of wine. No will power to speak of.

The pain made me weak and my insides screamed for the heavy dose of poison. Tears streamed down my face, mixing with the sticky sheen of sweat and pooling along the creases of my cracked lips with bits of sand that crunched between my teeth.

I could tip them over, but I was too selfish for that. And, to be honest, I wasn't sure I could trust myself not to lick the numbing juices from the floor. *Numbing*…the word soothed my soul with darkness, promising to take away the pain.

I weighed the possibilities of my near future if I remained in the clutches of Horus. Infection had begun, and it was only a matter of time before it was too far to cure. And Horus didn't strike me as the type to lend medical attention in any way. A day had already passed since he swooped down and stole me from Silas' arms. And no one had come to get me. The realization pressed down on me.

No one was coming.

With shaking hands, I reached over and wrapped my fingers around one of the red clay pitchers and brought it to my face. I closed my eyes and put it to my lips. It was so strong; the aroma burned my nostrils, but I kept drinking. Gulp after gulp until my stomach protested, and I ached for breath.

Warmth spread up from my belly, pulsed through my veins and stung my racing heart. My head lolled and tipped back to the wall, but I put the rim to my lips again and poured the last bit into my mouth. That was the last thing I remembered before crashing to the floor and sinking into darkness.

CHAPTER TWO

"Amun! Do we need to chain you up in the holding cells again, or are you going to listen to reason?" Anubis yelled at me from the edge of his chair.

My chest still heaved and burned from hours of running across the desert. When I'd watched in horror as my brother disappeared across the sky with Andie in his grasp, my legs moved before my mind even told them to. A foolish choice. I couldn't swiftly move from place to place as my cousin could, with his connection to the Underworld as a pivot.

It had taken most of the night, and when I could finally see Horus' palace in the near distance, five of his guards kindly informed me that Andie's head will be removed from her body if I dared step foot inside the building.

I wanted to believe it was an empty threat, but part of me wasn't sure. It'd been over a thousand years since I'd seen my petulant brother. Who knew what he was capable of now?

I paced the floors of Alistair's quarters while he sat with Anubis at a little table. They'd been muttering something while I toiled inside my own mind, but their words were futile. I couldn't will myself to calm down, let alone listen.

"You don't understand!" I replied, cutting off whatever reasoning they'd been throwing at me.

Anubis slammed a fist on the table. "Whether he kills Andie or not, going back there is exactly what he wants you to do!"

I ran fingers through my hair and pulled at it as I groaned. "All I hear are words preventing me from saving the woman I love."

He sprung from his seat. His onyx eyes fixed on me. "We can't storm over there without a plan."

My eyes bulged. "I don't care. Every minute that passes is a minute too long that my brother could be doing...God knows what to Andie." A shudder scratched through me. "His hands on her *body*, his mind in her mind. I can't just leave her there!"

Alistair let out a deep, raspy breath. "Silas, she's my daughter. Don't you think I want to flee to Horus and beg for his mercy? But I know I can't. We mustn't do this with haste. Not after everything she did to save you." The old man tipped his head to the side and looked at me with pity. "He won't kill her. He needs Andie to use against you."

I squared my jaw as my fists clenched at my sides. "Killing her would be a mercy. Keeping her alive is what I'm more worried about. If he gets inside her mind, who knows what he could make her do."

Anubis took a step back. "Yeah, or what he could discover about the colony and portal. But the Wise Man is right, cousin. Who's to say he won't just strike her down the moment he sees you? Then, not only would he have everything he needs from her mind, but he'll also have *you*. It would doom the people of the colony."

I knew he was right, but I battled internally with the rational part of my brain. When it came to Andie, I rarely stayed the course. Always veering off the path to follow her every whim, tugged along by my heartstrings. I'd do anything for that woman. But I also had a duty to so many…

I let a deep intake of air fill my lungs until they were tight, and I looked at my two friends. "We have until sundown to come up with a plan. Otherwise, I'm leaving to get her myself."

Alistair exchanged a glance with Anubis, then regarded me with a simple nod. "That's fair."

Before we uttered another word, I spun on my heel and

stomped out of the room. Down the winding stone-cased halls and through the colony toward Andie's quarters. I threw the loose hood of my cloak up around my face, careful to shield it from the eyes of any passersby. I couldn't chance anyone recognizing me down here. Not yet. Not when they all still believed Amun to be so threatening. I couldn't afford to cause a riot amongst the Star People when I had so much else at stake.

The life of Andie, for one.

I made it to her room, unscathed by onlookers, and pushed open the door. Her Tanin pet crouched on the bed, hunched over a mess of crumbs and food scraps. He peered up and growled at me, holding a chunk of bread protectively to his chest. *Wretched beast*. I rolled my eyes and shut the door as I began pacing the floors. My leg muscles burned with the strain I forced on them, unrelenting in the rage that coursed through my body.

My brother's face flashed in my mind; evil and sneering, his hands on the woman I loved. Fury seared across my chest and I hauled my fist back before firing it into a wall. Bits of stone crumbled to the floor from a crack that formed, and I winced.

"Fuck!" The word seethed from my mouth as I foolishly tried to shake the pain away from my hand. The skin lay torn across the ridge of my knuckles and blood already dripped from the ripped flesh. I could curse this mortal body sometimes.

Someone knocked at the door. I grabbed a dirty cloth from a pile in a wicker basket to wrap around my hand and opened it to find my cousin standing there with his familiar Niya at his feet. He presented in his human form, and I knew it was a white flag. I turned back into the room in a huff and he followed me.

Anubis glanced at the hole in the wall with a sigh. "I see you're making yourself at home."

I wrapped the towel around my hand tightly. No reply to be found.

"Amun, I'm worried about you—"

"You should be!" I snapped. But I took a deep breath and willed myself to calm. Anubis wasn't my enemy. A stumbled back a step, and a sob trembled through me. "I'm…losing my damn mind."

He took a seat on one of the stone benches. "Why would your brother take Andie and not you?"

I sat down and regarded him from across the table. "It's just another attempt to gain control over me. He saw us kissing right before he swooped down and took her. He knows she means something to me."

Anubis nodded slowly, the look of understanding spreading across his slick, dark features. "Something that's never happened before."

"Aside from our parents and you, Horus has had no

other sway over me. Nothing to dangle with threats." Another image flashed in my mind. Horus standing over Andie's bloodied body on the floor. My insides tightened. "I'm worried what he'll find in her mind, that he'll discover the location of the colony, the portal. But also…"

Anubis leaned forward, eagerness in his wide eyes. "What? Is this about where you've been all these years? Is that something you wish to keep from your brother?"

I could only nod. There was just too much explanation that came with that admittance.

Niya hopped up on the bed and Shadow growled at her, but the silky jackal ignored the creature and curled up for a nap. Anubis rubbed his chin in thought.

"You know, you can trust me," he said with all sincerity. I knew he was right. And I did, I trusted my cousin with my life. He was more of a brother to me than my own actual brother. "Horus isn't able to get in my head. Your secret would be safe with me."

Nerves twisted in my gut like brambles, but he was correct. In all the millennia of our existence, Horus had never been able to get inside the minds of our family. Perhaps it was because of their creation, their wholeness. Just another dreadful reminder of how incomplete I was. Forever tied to the soul that they made me from.

My brother's.

But Anubis was like a locked vault sitting before me,

ready to safeguard all the secrets that plagued my broken soul. But my time with Andie and Alistair in the future… it didn't plague me at all. It wasn't a scar on my life, rather…a bright light in all the darkness that my brother has cast over me all these millennia. My time with them was precious, something I held close to my heart. But I knew I could share it with Anubis.

"I rigged the portal for time travel," I admitted.

The skin between his brow pinched together. "I've pieced together vague bits of things Alistair had let slip. But…I couldn't bring myself to believe it. *Time* travel? Is that really possible?"

The words were hardly a whisper from his lips. But I nodded.

"Oh, it is," I assured him and leaned back against the wall while I nursed my knuckles, the blood already seeping through the cloth. "It took a while, but Alistair and I figured it out and we altered one keystone. I spent thousands of years trapped in my amulet, before Alistair found it and accidentally released me. When I'd discovered how long had passed and saw the state of the world centuries from now, I knew I had to come back here and fix it." I shifted and leaned forward in my seat. "Something happens here that affects the evolution of the beings on this planet. Star People are nothing but a myth, and no one knows what they truly are or what they're capable of."

I left it there, allowing my cousin the time to process it all. It was heavy. That I knew. Our kind have roamed the universe for millions of years, but never dreamed the concept of time travel. Never needed to. Time holds no value when you're immortal.

His gaze fell to the floor as he retreated inside his own mind.

"Do you…believe me?" I asked after the silence became too much to stand.

Anubis looked up and offered a smile. "Yes. Always. I'm on your side, Amun." His smile widened to a grin. "Or is it Silas now?"

I chuckled. "Both. Something in me recognizes *both* men. I've yet to experience that in all my lives." I rubbed my lips together in thought. "My life with Andie and Alistair, before we arrived here, it's not something I wish to share, nor is it something that can fall into the wrong hands."

"Like your brother's," he replied in agreement.

I shrugged. "It's the only thing I've ever had that's… *mine*. I hope to one day return home to it. In peace. But I just couldn't ignore my duty to come back here and fix what my brother has done or might do."

Anubis turned in his seat and raked his hands over his thighs in sudden frustration. "Aren't you sick of this? Millions of years, Horus has dictated almost everything you do. I mean, how many times have you guys killed one another? How is that any way to live?"

He was right. *Again*. I stood from my seat and slowly paced the floor between the table and bed. Andie's wretched pet bared his teeth every time I came near the mattress, but I ignored the beast. "I just, I carry this sense of guilt with me everywhere I go. Since my creation. I've always felt like I owed Horus something. A part of me. Flesh for flesh, and all that."

Anubis narrowed his eyes. "What your parents did is no fault of yours. Your creation is not something you should feel guilty over. You don't owe anyone anything."

I slowed my stride and glanced down at the two animals that sat on the bed. So oblivious to the perils of our lives. I wished for such bliss. The Tanin creature blinked those massive, bug-like eyes up at me with curiosity. Did he wonder where his beloved Andie was? Or did he know? I reached out to pet him, and he snapped his pointed teeth, narrowly missing my fingertips. But he quickly softened, thinly tolerating my touch when I began scratching at the skin between his ears.

Anubis stood and took a few steps toward me. "So, what do you want to do?"

A deep sigh billowed from my chest. "I need to get Andie back. Whatever the cost."

He crossed his arms. "Yeah? But then what? Let's just

say you succeed. You save Andie from the clutches of Horus and you both escape. How are you going to protect her from your brother for the rest of her life?"

It was time I faced the truth I knew had been there the whole time. I just didn't want to accept it. I looked to my loyal cousin and failed to hide the rush of broken emotions that surfaced as I pursed my lips, my eyes glossing over.

"I can't," I admitted quietly. "It's too dangerous for her to be here. She…" I stomped down the urge to change my mind. "Her and Alistair must go back."

CHAPTER THREE

The tendrils of a wine coma were so much heavier than a dream. Everything felt so real, so tangible. My hands gently slid through the damp grass beneath me as I buried my toes in sand. The body of water that stretched to the horizon, one long gone in my time, lapped about with the ebb and flow of the warm breeze.

I tipped my head back and sucked in a deep breath that filled my lungs with a sweet, mild air as two arms wrapped around me from behind. My heart fluttered at his touch. After so many years without him, the simple nearness of Silas sent my pulse soaring. But he rested his head against my back with a sigh, and I knew.

"You're saying goodbye again, aren't you?" I whispered over my shoulder.

Even in a dream, I knew something was wrong.

"Andie, I love you. Almost too much at times," his voice vibrated against my skin. "You'll never understand the sacrifices I'm willing to make just to keep you safe."

I turned in his arms and touched my palm to his worried face. Silas leaned into it. "And what about the sacrifices *I'm* willing to make? For you. For us." The rims of my eyes burned. "I'm not ready to let you go again."

He hugged me close, his lips on mine immediately. The taste of our tears touched my tongue, and I gasped for air. But Silas refused to let me go. Finally, he pulled back.

"I understand," he said in a breathy reply. "But, since only one of us is immortal, I can't bear the thought of keeping you in a line of danger just to appease my selfish heart."

I stared down at the little patch of grass between us, darkened by our shadow. I didn't like this dream anymore. But it was still better than the reality that faced me outside. I looked up and smiled through the tears.

"Well, if you're leaving me again, at least let me look at your face one last time. Etch it into my memory forever."

My fingertip traced all the beautiful, sharp lines of his face. Admiring the raw beauty of such a man. Unlike anyone I'd ever seen before. His skin was the color of wet sand drying in the sun and felt just as soft. His eyes dragged me in, sucking me into a hypnotizing void. Green and gold, my two favorite colors.

But the longer I stared, the faster they faded. Melding and morphing into a familiar empty glower. The milky walls of the dream sagged until they disappeared, and Horus' dark gaze fixed on me from just a foot away. But sideways. He grabbed my arms and sat me upright before propping me against the wall.

"There we go," he said with mock concern and futilely wiped the dirt from my clothes. "I thought you'd never wake up."

My stomach rolled immediately, empty of food and burning from the heavy dose of wine I'd downed earlier. The smell of my festering wounds mixed with ripe body odor filled my nostrils and a wave of nausea forced its way through me, pushing upward.

With a single glance to my right, I saw the empty overturned pitcher and guilt took over me. I leaned forward just as a sour liquid spewed from my mouth…and all over Horus' linen shirt.

"What the–" He jolted back and gawked down at the reddish-brown splotch on his clothes, his hands hovering helplessly in the air at his sides, and then glared at me from under his lowered brow. "I should make you *eat* this!"

A painful guffaw hiccupped from my chest and I wiped my mouth with the back of my hand. "Technically, I already did."

The stench of my own vomit swirled in the tiny space we occupied and sent another wave of dizziness washing over me. My head spun, threatening to black out, and I slowly fell over. But Horus hastily grabbed my arms and forced me into an upright position.

"Pull yourself together!" he demanded. "You've yet to tell me anything I need."

An agonized moan sputtered from me and he tightened his grip on my arms. I didn't like him this close. His nearness scratched under my skin and only reminded me of my situation; that I had nowhere to go. Nowhere to hide.

I strained for every breath as I glared at him. "Why don't you just take it from my mind like you do with everyone else? Why drag it out like this? You're just torturing us both."

His hands swiftly retreated, and I noticed his body stiffen. "It doesn't work like that."

"Yes, it does," I insisted. "Your brother told me all about how it works. You can seep into anyone's mind, get information. Sway their will to your own."

Horus looked away without a reply.

Then something struck me, a thought. A...*realization*. If I hadn't been in so much pain or inundated with alcohol, perhaps I would have noticed it earlier. The prying, the torture, the wine to loosen my lips.

A laugh grew in my empty belly and I let it spread.

Horus' sudden look of dismay only made me laugh even harder, and I nearly fell over in a delusional fit.

"What could possibly be so funny?" he asked spitefully, but with a hint of embarrassment.

"You–" I struggled through a laugh, "You can't do it. Can you? You can't control my mind."

His expression blanked. "I'll find a way."

Horus stood on his feet and I carried on with my fit of laughter as his leather sandals scuffed the floor of the cell. His fists clenched in balls at his sides. How could someone choose to live with such anger? Such hatred for others, and yet desire their love so badly?

I calmed the roll of chuckles and sagged against the wall behind me. Sweat covered my skin in thick layers, mixed with blood and dirt in areas. The blaring sun above, filling the cell from the open ceiling, didn't help.

"No, you won't," I replied. "And you know it. That's why you're so frustrated. Maybe if you spent your energy actually building trust and showing people *why* they should love you, rather than forcing their hand, you'd get somewhere."

He turned on his heel in a cloud of muttered grumbles and stormed out. I fell into a second wave of maddening laughter, stoked by the fading moans of frustration I heard follow Horus through the palace. In my final hours of agony, at least his aggravation brought me a bit of joy.

But I was feeling a slow disconnect from my dying body. My inner resolve slowly pulling away, leaving behind the pain and infection that I knew must flood my blood stream by now. My broken leg beneath the denim and leather of my pants was so swollen and throbbed with an intense heat. I ached to free it from the confines of the fabric, but I was too cowardly to move that much.

I glanced down at my tattoo, the handmade outline of an ankh, and thought about how strong Silas must have been to withstand the wrath of his brother for two years. Even without his mind fully intact, it must have been awful to endure those first few days. Or months. Or…who knew how long Horus had tortured his brother for information before realizing it had broken him.

I *had* to be strong. I had to hold on to the flimsy hope that one day I'd get out of here alive.

A recent memory flashed across the forefront of my mind. Eirik and me sitting in the Great Hall. Them telling me how the Venuvians aren't magic, they only tap into our body's natural ability to heal. And then Silas. Before his wretched brother swooped down and plucked me from his arms. How I'd watched that dying flower flourish in his hand.

You have the potential. It's born into you.

I had no clue how to tap into that. How to find my own ability to heal or even use it. But I had to at least try. What did I have to lose at this point? I was a goner soon anyway, if no one came to find me. If Horus didn't grow tired and let me go. But even if he spared me that mercy, I wouldn't get very far.

I spotted a small tear in my jeans, just below the knee and above the break in my tibia. Carefully, I poked two fingers inside and dragged it apart, widening the hole until it spread down the leg of my pants and I could finally free my broken appendage. The relief was palpable, and I stiffened against the scratchy wall behind me as I braced through the pain that came with the rush of blood that pulsed upward.

Like a woman in labor, I breathed through it, waited out the fresh sensation of agony. Imagining the sight of an injury like this is one thing, but actually seeing it with my own eyes was another. I struggled with the reality. The dark purple skin, tight and shiny. The thick, dark blood that oozed on the surface. The visual made me sick, and I fought my way through the desire to pass out. I wrapped my shaking hands around the area below my knee, mindful not to touch or disturb the break just below it.

"Okay," I said to myself. "You can do this. Just...*imagine* it?"

I felt a little foolish, but I knew it was possible. I'd seen it with my own eyes. Had it done to my body by others. I could rapidly heal; I could endure it. But could I evoke it?

With a deep, jittery breath over my trembling lips, I closed my eyes and focused on the festering wound. The jagged piece of bone that poked through the broken skin. I pictured it joining with the other end. The massive pockets of infection melting away. Over and over, I held the image in my mind. My hands warmed against the skin of my leg and I swear I could feel something working. Perhaps it was all an illusion, built on the flimsy hope that this could work. Or…

Maybe it actually was working.

Something sounded in the distance, deep in the palace. Voices arguing. Deep tones that were familiar, but they mixed under a muffled echo that the stone structure provided. I couldn't tell what they were saying, but it was heated. And it was a distraction.

An involuntary shake entered my body, and I struggled to keep my focus. Hours of torture paired with severe dehydration and a fatal wound had long since taken a toll. I held on as long as I could, with the very last ounce of my strength, but it wasn't enough. The strange energy I'd tapped into fizzled away, and the severity of my infliction sprung back like an elastic band.

Darkness closed in from all sides of my vision and pushed me down to the floor, forcing me against my will into another coma-like sleep. I fought back with what little I had left, floating in and out of consciousness as the sounds of rattling metal clamoured against my ears.

My cage was being opened.

Grimy strands of my hair partially blocked my view as I lay on the floor and peered up at a tall visitor, blocked out by the late afternoon sun that flooded the cell from above. The shadowed figure then knelt at my side and my blurred vision faintly picked out the familiar features of the man I loved.

"Silas?" I hardly whispered.

His fingers eased the hair from my face, and I wept at the pain I witnessed on his.

"What has he done to you?" he said in disbelief, his voice breaking with every word. I saw him glance at the empty pitchers of wine and mutter something under his breath.

I thought I replied, but no sound touched my ears and the blanket of darkness pressed down even harder. But I had to hold on; it was finally over. Silas was here to save me. His two able arms slid under my body and scooped me from the floor. But the pain was too much. I wrapped myself in the safety and comfort of his touch and gave in to the darkness. Let it take me away. Carrying with me the image of my savior into a vast field of emptiness where I waited for death.

CHAPTER FOUR

Reality dragged me from the depths of nowhere, as if I were being yanked by the neck through warm water until I finally broke the surface. Pain and agony were there to greet me. Like two mobsters standing over my grave, and I pried my parched tongue away from the roof of my mouth as I let out a moan.

There was a strange disconnect between my brain and body, and I wasn't sure if the last week had just been some horrible nightmare or not. The last concrete memory I could muster up was the image of Howard driving a knife into my gut. Slowly, my mind connected to my arm, and I shakily searched for the wound in my side, only to find a two-inch scar that was already mostly healed.

Which meant…

I blinked away the cloudy film that covered my eyes and assessed my surroundings. Jagged stone walls all around, a small table of medical supplies in the corner next to a few wooden crates. Shadow lay curled in a sleeping ball between my feet. Like a cat. That's when I noticed the brace around my leg from the knee down. Similar to a cast, but not the white plaster kind. No, this was made of metal rods wrapped tight to my mangled leg with linens. It hurt like hell, but at least the appendage no longer hung from my body at an unnerving angle.

The edges of my vision cleared and I tipped my face to the left to find Silas' body slack in a chair, sound asleep. Exhaustion was clear in the way the skin wrinkled around his closed eyes, even in rest, and intensified by the dark circles that rimmed them.

I fought through the fog in my head and, bit by bit, recalled the series of events that transpired over the last couple of days. Finally getting Silas back, only to be ripped from him by Horus. Dropped from the sky into a holding cell fit for a zoo animal. My leg breaking in half and the gut wrenching sound of the bone snapping like a thick, wet branch. And then…a blade to my throat.

A sickening chill shivered through me and I carefully reached up to my neck. When my fingertips whisked the texture of fresh linens, my eyes immediately filled with tears. He nearly killed me. A ball of nerves coiled in my throat and I let out a gurgled cough.

"Andie?" Silas croaked and blinked the sleep from his eyes as he bolted forward to the edge of the bed. "You're not supposed to be awake yet. Your wounds are still healing."

Instinctively, I chortled, but it just came out in a painful moan and I tried to shift in the bed. Just an inch to the side so I could partially turn towards him.

"So, what? They just keep everyone in a coma to heal?"

The space between his brows pinched together. "No. Only for wounds as serious as yours." He lowered his gaze disapprovingly. "Don't be stubborn."

"Me? Stubborn?" I joked weakly, but he didn't laugh.

He carefully took my hand in both of his and sighed as he held it to his face. The warmth of sleep seeped into my skin. "Not only did you snap your tibia completely in half, but it filled your blood with infection. You were severely dehydrated and suffering from alcohol poisoning." A tangible pain entered his glossy stare, and I had to look away. "What did my brother *do* to you?"

A flash of Horus with a thin blade to my throat bolted across my vision and my body raced with fresh fear. "I…I broke it when he dropped me from the sky." The words came out in dry cracks. "My God. I-It…must have been thirty feet…"

Silas squeezed my hand and I let out a wince.

"Sorry!" He immediately loosened the hold and gently kissed my fingertips. "I'll go get Eirik to put you under again."

"No, please," I begged. "It makes me feel funny. To come out of it, the darkness. I don't want to go back, I want to stay here with you."

Silas released my hands and settled back in his chair with a distant gaze that touched something beyond the space we occupied.

"What's the matter?" I asked. "Is everyone okay?"

He nodded solemnly. A weak attempt at a smile tugged at the sides of his mouth. "Everyone is just fine. Which is more than I can say for you." He shifted and leaned forward on the bed. "Andie, I think–"

Footsteps echoed in the doorway and Eirik entered with a surprise. "You're awake?" They glanced at Silas, but he just shrugged tiredly. My eyes followed them as they approached the other side of the bed and began examining the wounds. "I forgot how much of a tolerance you have for the sedation. You kept waking up before, too. When you first arrived."

I guffawed. "No surprise there."

I'd been heavily sedated for two years.

"What's that supposed to mean?" Silas asked me.

"Nothing," I said, and tried to hide the panic in my tone.

Shadow stirred at my feet and perked his head up, blinking widely at me. He carefully stepped over my body and crawled up the side of the bed toward my face. A gentle stream of coos purred in his throat.

"I'm fine," I assured him and scratched behind his ears. I flopped my head to the other side to find Eirik mixing things in a clay bowl with a pestle. "Come to use your magic healing powers on me?"

Eirik grinned as their slender white fingers worked the ingredients into a paste. "Hardly. Some would perceive it as a power, of sort, I suppose. But it's simply what we do. Venuvians heal. But we only use your body's natural ability to do so." They leaned over me to check the bandage on my neck. "We just speed up the process. You'll be good as new by morning."

"Thank you," I replied.

I tried to ignore the way Silas sat stiff and uncomfortable in the chair at my other side. I could see him in the corner of my eye, a hand over his mouth as he stared across the room, lost in thought. But I craned my neck to look at him fully.

"Speaking of superpowers." His eyes met mine as if I'd just interrupted a conversation he was having. "What was with that flower? How did you...*do* that?"

He crossed one leg over the other and smoothed a hand through his bed hair. "Like most of my family, I possess a certain power, yes."

"Like Horus' mind control ability?" I replied.

He only nodded.

"Can you…do that?" I asked. "Control minds? Have you…"

Silas stared at me unblinkingly. "If you're asking whether I've ever controlled your mind, the answer is most certainly not." I couldn't ignore the hint of offense in his tone. "Not only is that a power I don't possess, it's also something I would never do to you." He paused a beat and chewed at his lip. "Is that–did my brother find a way into your mind?"

I opened my mouth to answer, but Eirik set the clay bowl down on the table with a loud clang. "Perhaps I'll come back later and give you two some privacy."

Silas pushed off from the chair and stretched his back. "No need. I have some things to tend to. Stay, treat Andie. I'll come back later."

"You're leaving?" I asked with a little more desperation than I was comfortable with.

He smiled and leaned over my body to place a careful kiss on my forehead, then hovered there, staring into my eyes. Searching. The golden flecks peppered in the mossy green reflected off the light in the room and flashed with…something. A sadness that touched my heart with a strange sense of familiarity.

"Just for a bit," he promised. "I'll be right back."

He turned to leave as Shadow nudged at my hand for more head scratches, and I waited until the sound of his retreating footsteps faded out before I turned to Eirik.

"Something's wrong," I said flatly. "I can feel it. But what are the chances he'll actually tell me?"

Eirik began gingerly pulling at my neck bandages. "I'd wager the chances are as good as you telling him what truly happened during your time with his brother."

I sighed and mindlessly scratched at Shadow's ear. "So, slim, then."

***

"Are you eating?" Dad asked me as he stirred a steaming cup of tea.

"Yes," I assured him with a disgruntled sigh akin to that of a narked teenager. "Eirik force fed me eggs this morning."

I stood by the door to his room, eager to leave and get away from the prying questions. Was I eating? How did I feel? Was I tired? I'd had enough of that from both sides. And I knew they were only skirting around the real questions that they all itched to ask me.

About my time with Horus.

But I wasn't ready to talk about that. And, honestly,

I wasn't sure if I ever would be. I woke up this morning good as new, just as Eirik had promised. But it still felt weird to be upright and walking on a leg that had been snapped in half just a day ago. Silas sat at the quaint table set with Anubis, waiting for me to be ready to leave. Aside from that first initial moment after I woke up in the infirmary, he hadn't left my side since.

I motioned to the door with a cock of my head and he stood up, ready to go.

"Take it easy today, Peach," Dad told me.

Anubis, in his jackal form, turned in his seat. "And, if you remember anything…from before. Any details that Horus may have about–"

"He knows nothing about the colony or the portal," I said curtly and pursed my lips. "I swear."

Anubis' shoulders went slack with relief and he opened his mouth to pry further. But I spun around toward the door before he got the chance. "I'm heading back to my room."

"Oh, yes, of course," he replied, and I glanced over my shoulder to catch him exchange a look with my father before throwing me a toothy smile. "Feel better."

I nodded and left Dad's quarters with Silas in tow. *Feel better*. I laughed inside. Physically, I felt like I could run back to my room. The miracle work of the Venuvians was a wonder. As if I had never broken my leg to begin with. But mentally? Emotionally? I was beyond repair. My wounds may have healed overnight, but the internal ones were still fresh and warm.

We turned a corner in silence, and Silas tugged at my arm when the hallways divided into two paths.

"Shouldn't we go the long way around?" he asked.

"Don't be nervous about cutting through the Great Hall," I told him. "Dad, Eirik, and Anubis all said they'd spread the word that you're different now." I took his hand in mine. "A new man."

His returning smile didn't reach his eyes. "Quite literally."

I playfully pushed at his arm, but he yanked me close and I leaned against hist chest as he wrapped me in a tight embrace. I tipped my face up, taking a moment to admire his raw beauty before touching my lips to his.

"For the record," I whispered against his mouth. "I'd take you in any form. Amun, Silas, whatever your name is."

His hand cupped the back of my head and pulled me in for another kiss. This one slow and lingering, jogging my pulse.

"A name means nothing," Silas replied quietly. "Just know that I am yours. That's all that matters."

I searched his troubled eyes and my stomach toiled with unease. "Forever?"

Silas pressed his forehead to mine. "Always."

That burn of agitation never settled in my gut, but I ignored it as we strolled back to my room hand in hand. I was away from Horus. Safe and alive. I had my father and Silas back in my life and new friendships growing, which was a new experience for me. But I liked it.

So why couldn't I shake this sense of something… looming?

We entered my room to find Shadow perched on my table with some dried meat held in his tiny, clawed hands. He growled at Silas' outreached arm and chomped his teeth at the air between them.

I laughed. "He'll learn to love you in time."

Silas looked away and stood in the middle of the room, seemingly unsure what to do with himself. I opened the door again and pointed into the hall for Shadow. "Go see if there's anything left from supper," I told the creature. He hopped down to the floor and scampered out the door before I closed it.

In the silence of my room, I could hear the heartbeat I felt thrumming rapidly in my chest with worry. But I closed my eyes as two arms slipped over my waist and wrapped around me from behind. He kissed my neck, dragging his lips over the exposed skin. The feel of his body against mine was enough to calm my rampant heart, but then the vague memory of a lucid dream seeped into my mind's eye.

I turned in his arms and saw a sadness in his eyes. "Hey," I said and cupped his cheek. Just like in my dream, he leaned into it. "Why the long face? I'm here, I'm fine. *Alive*. I'm not going anywhere." His expression tightened. "Silas, what the hell is wrong? Tell me."

"Nothing. I just–" His eyes flitted back and forth, as if searching mine for a safe place to let down his words. "I just can't get the thought of my brother's hands on you out of my head."

That's what was bothering him? Aside from torturous intent, Horus never laid a finger on me in that manner, the way Silas clearly worried about. But I got it, now that I could look at it from another angle. My physical wounds were clear, Silas could see that much. Anyone could. But the unknowing, the inability to see what truly transpired in that cell must have been killing him.

"He didn't touch me," I said. "Not like that. I swear."

There was no relief in his stoic expression. "That doesn't help."

"Well," I replied cheekily and lifted my arms to wrap around his neck, pulling his mouth closer to mine. "Let's just replace it with a new image, then. How about *my* hands on *your* body?"

From his neck, I dragged my fingertips slowly down across his chest, to the hem of his linen tunic and lifted it over his head. Silas' lean muscles gleamed in the heavy candlelight of my room and I wasted no time in smoothing my palms over the soft ridges of his body.

He seemed hesitant at first, but within seconds I felt him soften in my arms and he reached around to cup my bottom in his hands before giving it a squeeze. Crushing me against him. A low rumble in his chest vibrated through mine and a warmth spread out from my center. I loved the way his body always reacted to mine, matched by my own desire.

His face nuzzled my ear, his breath tickling the skin. "You'll have to do better than that," Silas whispered, and a hot shiver ran down my spine.

A devilish grin smeared across my face and I pushed him down on the bed where he settled with a bounce. He peered up at me from under a lowered brow, heavy with want. He watched me peel the clothing from my body, slow and seductive, revealing my naked shape. I delighted in the sight of his manhood growing, his mouth gaping as wanting breaths spilled over his lips.

My bare legs touched his which dangled over the edge of the bed and I slowly crawled over him and rolled my hips forward. It drove a deep moan from Silas' chest, and I leaned down to whisper in his ear, "Challenge accepted."

CHAPTER FIVE

I rolled over onto my back and stretched my achy limbs; stiff from the deep, comfortable sleep I'd fallen into the night before. It was the most pleasant sleep I'd had since my arrival at this place. Free of worry. Free of pain or the sickening withdrawals of alcohol. I fell off my tiny wagon during my time with Horus, but the heavy dose of wine I'd had just days ago had no presence in my blood for some reason. The fact that I didn't lie in a puddle of sweat told me as much. But also, the new ability to take a deep breath, fill my lungs without protest. Or the fact that my hands no longer trembled. I still wanted a drink. Mentally. But *physically*...I felt renewed.

Perhaps Eirik added something to my treatment. I'd have to ask them when I got the chance.

I smiled up at the ceiling, drenched in this fresh sensation. Happiness. It had been too long since I genuinely felt it. I rolled over to wrap my arm around Silas, but only the chill of empty bedding met my embrace, and I swatted the sudden rush of panic that entered my chest. He was probably just getting food.

I inched toward the foot of the bed and slipped out, suddenly hyper aware that I was stark naked and definitely grateful for the gift of a door. I hauled on my newly mended pants and rifled through my bag for the tank top I knew was in there. I was thankful I'd stuffed a couple in my bag before catching my flight, but if I were staying here, I'd need new clothes soon. I'd also been meaning to restock my supplies with rations for a while now, so I threw on my backpack before heading out through the colony in search of Silas.

I followed the scent of breakfast until the sounds of early risers echoed through the halls. I emerged in the Great Hall to find it bustling with the morning crowd. The feline Mau people gathered around a group of tables while a few Nuvi worked behind the long counter near the front of the massive space. God, their dark skin and gilded veins were simply stunning. Like works of art.

I stood near the mouth of the opening and admired the way the gold caught the natural light that filtered down from the ceiling. I crossed my arms as I scanned the room, noting other beings other than the Mau and the tall, pale Venuvians. Creatures that took on human-like qualities but were clearly not of this planet. Skin of various shades of green, blue, even red. Some with hair that looked like copper wires, while others had no hair at all. Pointed ears and toothy grins. This was a colony, a haven, but also a home. A hub for beings of every walk of life, living in harmony. But they shouldn't be forced to stay down here. They all had a right to the world above, just as much as the people of Earth.

Horus had to be stopped.

I let out a sigh, still tired and yearning for the comforts of my warm bed, curious where Silas had run off to. But I approached the stone counter that divided the Nuvi cooks from the rest of the Great Hall and smiled when one of them turned to look at me.

"Good morning," they said. A tall man with wide-set eyes. "Hungry?"

"I think I'll just get a tea for now," I replied. He nodded and spun around to fetch a clean mug for me. "You guys are wonderful cooks," I added, surprised at myself for the sudden desire to strike up a conversation. "To prepare food for all the different people down here, food they all like."

He set the clay mug down in front of me and smiled. "You should see the farm. One of our goats just had a calf and fifty new chicks hatched yesterday morning. Our corn harvest is going to be great this year, too."

He grabbed a large metal tea pot and filled my mug.

"How do you grow crops down here?" I asked him. "Without the sun."

He pointed up at the ceiling where the sunlight mirrored through periscopes shone down and lit up the room. "Just like that. Only bigger."

I took my steaming mug. "I'll have to come see it sometime," I said.

He brightened. "Yes, please do."

I held out a hand. "I'm Andie, by the way."

The man shook it firmly. "Darius. And I know who you are." He grinned. "Everyone down here in the colony knows who you are."

My cheeks filled with heat and I stepped back. "Oh, really? Is that…bad?"

Darius chuckled and tossed a small towel onto his shoulder. "It's good. Don't worry."

I said goodbye and turned to face the packed hall as I strolled over to a small empty table near the back. Shadow appeared and hopped up on the seat next to me, a half-eaten bun in his hand. He held it out in an offer.

I held my warm mug close to my chest and sighed happily. "Thanks, buddy. But it's all yours." I took a sip of my tea. "Hey, do you know where Silas is?"

Shadow stopped chewing and blinked his large black eyes up at me. One of his little hands touched the skin of my arm and I felt that same warmth as before, when he was trying to tell me something.

"Go see my dad?" I asked, but the creature just continued eating his snack.

I finished my tea and headed off toward Dad's quarters. Just as I approached the closed door to his room, it opened with a loud creak and my father stepped out into the hall, a backpack slung over his one arm. He regarded me with surprise.

"Oh, morning, Peach," he said and closed the door behind him. "I was just coming to get you."

"Have you seen Silas?" I asked. "What's with the bag? Going somewhere?"

Dad patted my arm with a sigh. "Come with me."

My nerves crawled slow and cautious under my skin as I hesitantly strolled behind him. He led me down even more corridors I'd yet to see before and with every step my heart rose higher and higher in my throat.

"Dad, where are we going?" I asked nervously. "Where's Silas? What's going on?"

"I'll explain it all when we get there," he replied solemnly.

"Get *where*?"

He sighed. "Just follow me."

We walked in silence, aside from the repetitive patter of our boots against the dirt floors beneath us. Something was wrong. I could feel it in my bones. Not just from the way my father refused to give me more than a few words and danced around any sort of reply, but also in how a sense of familiarity tickled the back of my mind. These particular halls, this direction–plunging further underground–I'd been here before.

Finally, his pace slowed, and I sidled up next to him as we emerged onto a large balcony of sorts. It overlooked a massive cavern, perfectly carved out in the shape of a square. As if we stood inside a giant cube. The ceiling towered above us, and the impressive space stretched out and around. Runes and glyphs covered every square inch of stone. Ones…I'd surely seen before. I noted the stone stairway to the left and a sense of a memory pinged in my brain. I glanced down at the toes of my boots, just inches from the edge. A metal railing preventing me from falling over.

This time.

This was the pit. The portal. The place where Howard left me for dead and I got sucked back in time.

Dad took a few steps down and turned to look up at me in wait. "Come down with me, Peach."

"No," I said in a choked whisper and slowly backed away. "Why would you bring me here?"

Dad pursed his lips and held out a hand. "Andelyn–"

"*Where* is Silas?" I demanded, my eyes bulging from the anger that pushed at them from behind.

"It's time for us to go," he replied sadly.

"Go where?"

He waited a beat and then glanced down at the circle at the bottom of the pit. "Home."

I knew it.

"I already am, Dad," I argued. "Here. With you and Silas."

He moved up a step and held onto the railing as he pleaded with his eyes. "It's not safe for you here. It never was." He reached out with his other hand. "Please, let me take you home."

I slapped his hand away. "Don't you fucking dare!" Tears swelled and spilled down my cheeks. "Silas is my home!"

"You think I want to go back?" he bellowed, his voice smashing against the walls around us as he moved up one step. "You think I want to leave all this behind? This is my *life*, Andelyn. Everything I've worked for is here, and more. But *your* life is the most important thing to me."

I guffawed and crossed my arms in defiance. "And how do you expect to explain our sudden reappearance to the world? You've been gone for over two years, Dad. And let's not forget that Howard *murdered* me. I don't even have proof, the wounds are only a couple of weeks old, but they look like they healed years ago."

"We'll figure it out," he said without an ounce of confidence. He knew I was right.

I tapped my boot against the floor. "I'm not going anywhere."

"You don't get a choice in the matter," he seethed.

"I am not a god damn child!" I yelled back. "I *do* get a choice and I choose to stay here with Silas!"

"*Silas* is the one who made me do this!" Sweat beads broke out on his wrinkled forehead, and I immediately saw the regret in his pained expression. He wasn't supposed to tell me that.

Then I realized…Silas had just strolled right into that cell and scooped me up, walked out of his brother's palace with ease. No fight, no Horus to stop us. Then, after we got back, his strange and distant behaviour. The familiar sadness he carried with him. As if he were leaving me again. But he wasn't. Not this time. *I* was the one leaving.

So, where was the coward now?

I remembered then, the angry voices I'd heard before he fetched me from the cell. I thought about that for a moment, then tipped my head back as I let out a maniacal laugh. "I'm going to kill him. He traded himself, didn't he? For me."

I looked at Dad and his reluctant, gentle nod was all the

confirmation I needed. I couldn't believe it. I'd risked my life to save the man I loved. Did everything in my power to fix him, to bring him back to me. And he just waltzed back into the arms of the enemy before shipping me off to the future.

Without him.

CHAPTER SIX

"Andelyn!"

I wretched my arm from my father's grasp. "Absolutely not! You can stay here and be a coward, but I'm going to get him." My watery eyes pleaded for him to understand. "Dad, Silas is our *family*." I squared my jaw. "He may be a total freaking idiot, but he belongs with us. Just as much as he does to these Gods."

Dad's shoulders slumped. "Don't you think I know that?"

I stood, arms crossed in defiance, and my eyes flashed. "I'm going."

He stuck his hands on his hips. "And what about the safety of the colony? Of the hundreds of people who live here?"

I placed my palm over my heart as guilt touched it. "I ran away at first because I didn't understand what this place was and, when I found you and discovered Silas was alive, I acted rashly." I shook my head. "But this isn't rash, I swear. I would never put these people in danger now. Horus tried relentlessly, but he can't get inside my head." I sucked in a breath of confidence. "I don't plan on getting caught, but if I do, there's no risk to the colony *or* the portal."

Dad mulled it over in anxious silence, his mouth pursed in thought. He looked at me and adjusted his glasses. "And what about…your issue?"

My eyes widened. "My *issue*? You mean the drinking?" I crossed my arms again and tightened my fists underneath. "It's under control."

He shook his head. "I still don't think you should go. It's too dangerous."

"That's really for me to decide, though, isn't it?" I pulled at the straps of my bag, securing it across my shoulders as I turned. "I'll be back soon."

"Jesus Christ, Andelyn!"

I sped off down the hall as the sounds of my father's voice calling my name faded away. Hot blood pumped in my ears. I couldn't believe the nerve of them. *Both* of them. The more I thought about the hours since Silas saved me from the horrible fate, the more I could see now. How he just waltzed right in, no fear of being caught by his brother because there was no fear being had. He'd made a deal. Then his behaviour after I woke up. Distant, calculated. Exactly how he was the night before he and Dad left on the expedition two years ago.

I should have known. I should have figured it out before it was too late.

Now here I was, running back into the face of danger, nothing but spite and rage fuelling my every step. For Silas to just hand himself back like that, after everything we did to save him, it was like a slap in the face. If his brother hasn't killed him yet, he's going to pray for death when I get my hands on him.

I bypassed the Great Hall where I knew people would be gathered and veered off through one of the many tunnels that skirted around it. I needed to reach the Grand Entrance before my father sent someone after me. Or would he even bother? I'd done nothing but beg for my independence for years. Would this finally be the moment he gives it to me?

I rounded a corner and smacked right into a rock-hard body. Like colliding with a marble statue. My feet stumbled backward, but I found my balance and looked up to find Eirik with Shadow in tow.

"Andie," they said with surprise. "Where are you going? Is everything alright?"

I chewed at my lip as I scanned them for any sign of deceit. "Did my father send you after me?"

"Your father?" Eirik's face twisted in confusion, but it was too forced. They were terrible at lying, perhaps a trait of their people. They heaved a sigh. "Yes. In haste, he spared the details but said you'd need help."

I shook my head in frustration and kicked at the stone wall, grateful for my thick leather boots because it probably would have broken my toe otherwise. Bits of sand sprinkled to the floor, and I paced back and forth where I stood.

Shadow scampered over to me and let out a stream of disgruntled chirps.

"You know exactly what I'm doing," I told the creature.

"And what is that?" Eirik asked and took a careful step toward me.

My heart thrummed angrily in my chest. "Don't you think it's weird that Silas just scooped me up from his brother's palace and brought me back here? Without a care in the world."

Eirik's pale expression went distant as they thought for a moment. Then they shrugged. "I didn't really think about it. I was just thankful for your safe return."

"He traded himself for me," I replied. "He brought me back, made sure they healed me, then ordered my father to take me–" I forgot no one was supposed to know what Silas did, how he rigged their precious portal for time travel. Now that I thought about it, they must have all assumed I came from off-planet. I rubbed my lips together as I paced again. "He, uh, tried to send me back to where I came from while he trotted off into the arms of his brother."

Eirik's wide eyes bulged as a quiet gasp puffed from their mouth. "Goodness. What a foolish thing to do."

"Exactly!" I said, exasperated. "I can't let him do this. So, I'm going."

They leaned forward, their expression gawking in disbelief. "To Horus's palace? No wonder your father insisted I follow you."

"Oh, no, no, no." I waved my hand in the air. "You're not coming. It's too dangerous."

"Precisely the reason I *should* come," they insisted.

"I'm leaving right now," I said, hoping to cause delay.

Eirik straightened their back and smiled proudly as they tightened the sash that held their flowy grey robe in place. "Then it's a good thing I'm ready to go."

I strange sense of…something warmed my chest. No one, aside from my father and Silas, ever went to bat for me like this. I'd never truly had friends. Ever. I spent my whole life hand-in-hand with my dad as we travelled the globe. And I happily did so, there's nothing about my upbringing that I would change for the world. But having *this*, the feeling of friendship, the safety of knowing someone was there…

…I liked it.

I let out a defeated sigh and glanced down at Shadow. "Don't suppose I can convince *you* to stay behind, can I?"

Thin lids skimmed over his massive black eyes as he blinked up at me, then he shook his head, causing those cute dog-like ears to flap about. I laughed to myself and closed my eyes as I sucked in a deep breath. I was running out of time. I looked at Eirik and smiled.

"Fine, then." I cocked my head in the exit's direction. "Let's go."

***

I considered using the portal doors to teleport straight to Horus' palace, but two thoughts made me second guess it. We wanted to get in and out unscathed, but I had no idea where the portal doors were in the palace, so using them might land us right in the hands of the God of Vengeance. Also, I wasn't completely confident in my ability to use them. Sure, I'd been to the palace enough to visualize it in my head, but what if it worked differently? What if I portaled us right back into the cell that had held me? The safest route was the long trek across the expanse of desert that stretched between the colony and Horus' palace.

So, that's what we did.

It had already been well over two hours since we first began the journey and the hot late morning sun baked my skin. One of the few patches of oasis was just a few yards up ahead, and I longed for some shade. When my boots touched the lush green grass, I plunked down and grabbed the water canister from my bag and took a long swig. Shadow scuttled over to the edge of a small creek and lapped at the trickling water.

"You should cover your head," Eirik said and pulled at one of the many lengths of fabric that made up their beautiful robe-like cloak and tore it from a seam. "Here, allow me."

They knelt at my side and fashioned the grey silken scarf around my head, letting it drape down over my neck and shoulders. Despite being exposed to the sun for a better part of the morning, the material felt cool to the touch.

I pulled it through my fingers. "What's this made of?"

Eirik lowered their hood. "It's from my home planet. A substance generated from a plant called Choka. It has natural cooling abilities. We have material that self-warms, as well. Made from another plant called Thoka."

I admired how it had a slight sparkle in the sunlight that filtered down through the trees. Like fresh snow on a warm winter's morning. Something I never noticed before, down in the dull exposure of the colony. "I bet your planet is beautiful."

Their usually cheerful expression faltered. "It was. Once."

I took another sip of water and wiped my mouth with the back of my hand as Eirik sat down next to me.

"What happened to it?" I asked.

"Tanin miners came and harvested our resources until there was nothing left." Eirik's silver eyes blanked as they stared off in the distance. "Subtly at first. Then they came in droves, relentlessly taking whatever they wanted. Using my people's non-violent demeanor to their advantage. They sucked our planet dry." Eirik looked at me. "And we let them."

My heart ached for my friend. I'd had no idea. And to think that the rest of the universe was no better than the greed that will eventually fester on this planet made me even sadder.

"I'm sorry," I said. "That must have been awful." Shadow pushed at my arm with his head, forcing his way into my lap. I scratched behind his ears. "Tanin. Like Shadow?"

Eirik smiled at my pet. "Yes. Of sorts. The Tanin are an old race, with many facets and abilities. They cast their DNA across the entire universe and evolved differently on each planet it took root on." They cooed at Shadow in my lap as if he were a baby. "Thankfully for us, this one evolved to be a pleasant creature."

Shadow's body thrummed with a cat-like purr in my hands, and I chuckled.

"What's your home planet like?" Eirik asked me.

My heart skipped a beat, and I flew into a panic as my mind raced to form an acceptable response. "Uh, its…a lot like this one. Only…more heavily populated. Great cities cover almost all the land."

"That sounds like a spectacular sight."

I shrugged. "Not really. I mean, yeah, it looks cool, but the beauty of our past is almost non existent. I spent my entire life travelling around with my dad to uncover great treasures and buried history. Our job was to keep things intact, to remind our people of where we came from."

But what fools we were. The people from my time don't know what we truly are or where we came from.

"A noble duty, it sounds like," they replied proudly.

Talking about it gave me a ping of sadness that I didn't want to deal with right now. Part of me, deep down, missed my time. The simplicity of it all. The truth was, I'd go back, but only if Dad and Silas came with me. Shadow hopped off my lap, and I stood up to brush the moist dirt from my bottom.

"We should get going," I said.

Eirik stood with me. "Yes, of course. We're nearly there. I can see the tip of the palace in the distance."

Just as my boots touched the hot sand around the oasis,

a dark blanket of shadow moved overhead, and I glanced up to find two winged guards swoop down from the sky. The same ones that carted me off the first time I'd ventured this way. They landed in the sand with a heavy thump.

I widened my stance and braced myself. Shadow growled from behind the cover of my leg as Eirik held one of their long arms out in front of me protectively. I appreciated the intent, but a non-violent healer wasn't exactly the ideal bodyguard.

"Get lost," I told the two bird-headed men.

"You're in no position to be making orders," one of them thundered.

Shadow clawed at my pants and I scooped him into my arms. I tapered my eyes at the guard who spoke. "I'm not going anywhere with you."

"We don't intend to take you." He exchanged a devious glance with his partner. "Lord Horus has instructed us to keep you away from the palace." He paused to let his beaked mouth curve into a sneer. "At any cost."

My breath caught in my throat as he took a step toward me but, in a flash so swift I nearly missed it, Eirik's arm shot out and collided with the guard's chest, sending him soaring back at least ten feet where he slammed to the ground.

I looked at my friend in disbelief, but their mirrored expression told me they were just as surprised as I was. Eirik gawked at their own hands, as if seeing them in a whole new light, and flexed their fingers in awe.

The other guard closed in from my right and I backed away. Shadow squirmed in my arms, but I wouldn't let him go. Not now, not when this guy could so easily stomp on him. But he wouldn't relent. The lizard creature protested and pushed at my tight embrace as the guard neared us. Eirik moved to my side and tugged at my sleeve, motioning for me to get behind them. But Shadow's little body convulsed and expanded in my hands like a balloon before he squeezed the air out in a massive flame.

"Ahh!" I screamed while the heat reflected on me as if I were holding a flame thrower.

Shadow kept going, pushing out long powerful flames toward the guard until the white feathers of his wings caught fire. We stood in shock as the man flapped about, trying to douse the flames, but they continued to spread, and he took to the skies. His partner scrambled to his feet and followed him, leaving the three of us standing there in utter amazement.

My jaw hung open; my unblinking stare fixed on the quickly disappearing guards in the distance. "What. Was. *That*?"

"It appears your Tanin pet can breathe fire," Eirik replied.

Shadow hiccuped and a puff of smoke squeezed from

his throat.

"Did you know he could do that?" I asked.

They shook their head. "No, he's never shown abilities like that." They examined their own hands, stretching out both arms and flexing admiringly. "As for me…"

"You said the Venuvians are a peaceful, non-violent race?" I answered.

Eirik nodded innocently. "That we are. We're sworn to do no harm. Yet are built with these large, able bodies. Clearly I have a lot to learn about my own abilities."

"Well, whatever the reason, I'm grateful you were with me."

They seemed unnerved by this new discovery. "Perhaps, for now, we keep this information between us. I'm not sure…" Eirik pressed their lips together in thought. "I don't wish to know how others of my kind will choose to see this. They are already uneased by my fascination with other cultures. The languages, adapting my vocal chords."

"Really?" I guffawed. "Seems a little dramatic, if you ask me. You should be able to defend yourself."

Eirik shook their head. "Venuvians are experts at ensuring we don't insert ourselves in situations where we'd need to."

I patted their arm. "Well, your secret's safe with me." I inhaled deeply and cast my gaze to the distance where I knew Horus' palace awaited. "But we should get going.

Those two guards are going to make this harder than it has to be. Horus will be waiting for us."

"We'll have to be extra careful," Eirik replied. "Should we wait until the fall of night to sneak in?"

I chewed at my lip anxiously. "No. That will only give him more time to prepare. We have to go now if we want any chance at all."

We bounded toward the line of the palace where it cut the sky. I began this formidable journey to save Silas with nothing more than rage and will power to fuel me. But now, with time to consider what I was really doing, fear rankled in my chest. I was walking right back into the arms of the man who'd, just days ago, tortured me to the brink of death. I thought Silas was a fool for going back…

But what did that make me?

CHAPTER SEVEN

We skirted the edge of the sand dune that protectively semi-circled around Horus' palace and peered down at the stone property. At first glance, it looked like a busy shopping center with bodies bustling about. Not at all what it was like during my time here. My cell looked out onto the courtyard, the center of it all. And I didn't see a single other soul while I lay there on the floor.

"There's too many people around," I said.

Eirik's eyes scanned about. Then they stretched their arm and pointed. "There. Around the back. It's an open window on the main level. If we can get down the side of this dune without being seen–"

"We can!" I touched their arm. "I know a way. Follow me."

We snuck around the edge until the window was directly below us. We just had forty of fifty feet to decline first. I sat down in the sand and looked up at Eirik.

"I used to do this all the time when Dad and I were set up in a desert area for a while. For fun." I tucked my knees to my chest and inched towards the edge. "Use your back as a slide and you'll zip right to the bottom."

Shadow scampered over to me and chirped worriedly. I loosened my legs to create a cradle in my arms.

"Come on," I said and held him tightly when he crawled into my lap.

I lifted my feet and rocked back as I inched toward the edge, then spilled over and slid all the way to the bottom of the dune. My hair flapping behind. It was a bit of a rush and, as the pleasant memories of my childhood blinked through my mind, I stifled the urge to let out a *wahoo!*

When I came to a stop, in the chilly shadow of the back of the palace, I pushed to my feet and turned to watch Eirik's stark white figure rocket all the way down. The second they touched the bottom, they barrel rolled and sprung to their feet, their expression bursting with glee.

"Shhh," I whispered and put a finger over my lips.

Eirik lowered their head. "That was exhilarating."

"I know." I grinned, but then glanced around. "We have to stay quiet, though. If Silas is being held prisoner, then he's probably in the cells near the courtyard. Let's sneak in this window and get as close as we can to wait out the crowd of people. They can't stick around forever."

Eirik nodded. "Lead the way."

I carefully lifted my leg over the low open sill and stepped inside the palace. It was a dim and empty room, filled with bookshelves and tables with open texts splayed about. I crept toward the closed door and opened it a crack as Eirik kept close to my back. I slowly peeked my head out and glanced up and down the hallway.

"All clear," I whispered over my shoulder and opened the door all the way.

We tiptoed through the corridors, winding around corners and slipping into dark doorways whenever footsteps could be heard. Finally, we neared the courtyard, the center of the palace. We hid behind one of the many massive columns that lined the perimeter while people—servants—busied about.

The open ceiling let warm light fill the space and bathed the luscious greenery in sunshine. A large stone fountain trickled water in and over itself from the center, splashing over the rim of its circular basin onto the intricate stone tiled floor. Carvings masked every surface, highlighted with colors of teal and red with bits of gold. Images of other Gods and creatures, mostly avian in nature. Horus definitely had a swanky pad; I'd give him that. But one detail befuddled me.

The holding cells were gone.

The wall along the back, where a handful of cells once were, was now a solid expanse of brick. As if they were never there to begin with. That made little sense. My forehead pinched, and I turned to Eirik.

"I don't get it," I whispered. "The cells are gone."

"Are you certain this is where you were?"

I pursed my lips together and took another look around. "Yes, definitely. But how do you make something like that disappear? I-I don't know where else he'd be keeping Silas."

A yelp escaped my throat as a hand grabbed hold of my arm and wrenched me around. Eirik spun, too, and we faced the very person we came to save. But he didn't look thrilled to see us.

"What are you *doing* here?" Silas barked.

"We've come to rescue you," Eirik chimed in, oblivious to his sour mood.

His eyed widened with a fiery disbelief and he fixed his gaze on me. "Why didn't you go home?"

I yanked my arm from his grasp. "Go *home*? I can't believe you would just ship me off like that! As if I mean nothing to you!"

He took a panicked glance from side to side. "Keep your voice down." He sighed, but it did nothing to calm his seething anger. "Andie, you mean *everything* to me.

That's why I did it. Do you think it was easy for me to say goodbye to you *again*?"

I shook my head, fighting back tears. "But you didn't say goodbye. You made me think everything was okay, and you disappeared. Like a coward." Shadow wrapped his tiny arms around my leg, and I felt a warmth seep through my pants. He was scared and worried. "I knew something was wrong. I can't believe you'd just waltz back to your brother after everything we did to save you. After everything I went through."

Silas pinched the bridge of his nose. "Go, Andie. Now. Before my brother discovers you're here and extracts even more information from your mind."

"What?" I replied. "No, he can't. I didn't get the chance to explain it all to you, but he can't get in my head."

His face softened with relief as he looked at me, a hint of hope in his eyes. "Are you sure?"

I nodded. "Yes. He tried and tried, but it wouldn't work. That's why he…" Speaking of the events trudged up the still-fresh memories of the torture Horus inflicted on me. I mindlessly reached up to my neck. The wound now gone, but the emotional scar would forever be there.

Silas gripped my arms and forced me to meet his pointed stare. "Listen to me. Leave this place." He regarded Eirik for a second. "If he can't control her mind, then she's useless to him. He'll just kill her."

My friend stiffened and gave me a torn and pleading look of helplessness.

I shook desperately. "No, don't listen to him." I wiggled from Silas' grasp and narrowed my eyes at him. "I'm not a child. And I demand to know what sort of deal you made with your brother to get me out of here."

He took a step away and tossed his head back with exasperation. "I willingly offered myself to Horus if he agreed to let you go. Alive. And to give me time to make sure you were safe and healed. I swore to return to him."

I punched him in the arm. "Are you freaking kidding me?"

He rubbed at the spot I jabbed. "I couldn't be sure what my brother extracted from your mind! So, I arranged to have the portal destroyed after Alistair took you home. So, Horus could never use it for…" Silas threw a nervous sideways glance at Eirik. "For what I altered it to do."

A brazen smile spread across my face. "The portal is safe, I swear. Your brother couldn't get inside my head."

"A slight setback, indeed," another voice sounded from a few feet away. My heart jumped into my throat and I spun around to find Horus sauntering his way toward us. "But I'll find a way in, eventually." His conniving grin unnerved me as he circled around our little group like a predator stalking its prey.

"Brother," Silas replied dutifully, his arm stretched out

across my front protectively. "Apologies. I had no idea she'd come back. I'll make sure she's gone."

Horus ignored his sibling's plea and fixed his stare on Shadow at my feet. His dark eyes flashed. "A Tanin seedling? My, I didn't think any took root here on Earth. What an interesting notion." He clucked his tongue at me. His carefree act sicked me. "I'd watch out if I were you. It may be cute now, but they grow up to be monsters." He grimaced in Eirik's direction for a second. "Just ask the Venuvian." He then leaned toward me and my nerves ran cold with fright. "Trust me. If you think *I'm* bad, then you'd never survive a run-in with a full grown Tanin. Even with earthling DNA to water it down."

I could feel the anxiousness that tightened Silas' body, it practically hummed over the surface of his skin. The way his back stiffened like a board, his feet spread, ready to defend me.

"Horus, allow me time to escort Andie away from here, please."

The mentally unstable god examined his brother's face with a stoic demeanor as an awkward and tense silence fell around us. My heart raced as I waited for...*anything*. For someone to speak or make a move. Finally, Horus let out a loud chuckle that cut through the air and my stomach flopped when his calculating stare fixed on me.

"Where have you been all my life?" He jabbed a thumb

in Silas' direction. "Controlling my brother has never been easier. He's never been so compliant. So…willing." Horus tucked his hands behind his back and stepped away. He grinned at Silas. "Why don't you ask your dear Andie to join us for the party tonight?"

"Absolutely not!" Silas replied through his teeth.

Horus' expression quickly morphed to spite, further solidifying his status as unhinged. He couldn't be trusted, that much was evident. And now there was something he wanted. *Me*, to come to this party. And his brother stood in his way.

"You challenge me?" he tested.

Silas's arm flexed, and he pushed me farther behind him. Eirik shifted closer to me, bracing, ready to yank me from this tense situation at the drop of a pin. I didn't want anyone to get hurt, that's not what I came here for. I opened my mouth to relent, but Silas beat me to it.

"No," he replied sadly, and his shoulders slumped.

Akin to the way a child's mood changes on a whim, Horus suddenly beamed and clapped his hands together. "Excellent! Your precious Andie will join us this evening." He gawked at the length of Eirik. "The Venuvian scum is not invited."

My fists clenched as an unexpected ball of anger rolled in my gut. "If my friend can't come, then neither will I."

Horus drastically rolled his eyes and his head lulled to

the side to scrutinize his brother. "I see why you like her." An exaggerated sigh deflated from his chest. "Very well. The Venuvian can come. But we must dress you both for the occasion." He snapped two fingers at a passerby, a servant woman, and he placed a firm hand on their shoulder. "Take these two away to meet with the seamstress and have them dressed for the event."

The woman nervously bowed her head and motioned for us to follow. I hesitated, waiting for a cue from Silas to tell me to run. That he'd follow and we could escape this place. But he remained still. A pained look evident in his tortured expression.

With Eirik and Shadow in tow, I followed the woman down the echoed hall. I glanced over my shoulder where the two brothers stood watching us leave. One bouncing with disturbing joy, the other stiff and distressed as he stood as still as a statue. His glossy eyes never blinking, never leaving mine as I put more distance between us. As I turned a corner, I wished Silas could read my mind, so I could tell him I loved him and that everything would be alright. But I knew, just as I was sure he did, that would be a lie. He disappeared behind the wall and I immediately flew into panic-mode.

What have I gotten us into?

CHAPTER EIGHT

They led us to a far room to the more Eastern side of the palace. The servant woman ushered us inside and then closed the door, locking it before she disappeared back down the hall. Shadow scurried over to the window and sat on the wide sill while looking down at the chasm below. No escaping that way, I guess.

I turned to Eirik. "Don't suppose flying is one of your hidden abilities, is it?"

They frowned and stood in the center of the room. "Afraid not."

I spun around and examined the room. It was massive, housing a wide canopy bed adorned with blankets of silken textures mixed with furs. Stunning artwork plastered across the walls, depicting scenes of Horus standing with

Ra, the Sun God, while crowds of people worshipped at his feet. I guffawed and plucked one of many trinkets from a table. A golden figurine of a bird.

"He sure likes the finer things in life, doesn't he?" I said.

"It appears that one of those finer things is you right now," Eirik replied. "Amun was right. If Horus can't get inside your mind, then you're useless to him. But that's not the case. He sees value in you, in the way he can use you to control his brother."

I rubbed my hands over my exhausted face. "I don't know if that's a good thing or a bad thing." I hugged myself tightly and shook my head. "God, right about now is when I'd devour an entire bottle of vodka."

"Is that what you call your affliction?" Eirik asked as they swayed over to the large open archway and peered down at the expanse below.

A sigh tumbled from my chest. "It's my preferred drink of choice. Like wine. Where I come from it's consumed just as much as wine, anyway."

They gave me a puzzled look. "Where *do* you come from?"

My mind stumbled over words. The right words to say. Obviously, I'd said too much in the presence of Eirik, enough to spark their curiosity. But I didn't want to hide anymore. I was sick of keeping this a secret, and I ached to tell someone. But I knew divulging that information would only endanger my friend's life.

I settled with, "Somewhere far away."

Eirik chuckled. "I gathered as much. The strange way you use your words, the garments you arrived in, your odd connection to the Gods—"

"I don't have any connection to the Gods," I cut in. "Only Silas. I mean…Amun." I shook my head tiredly. "Whatever you want to call him."

"But you were apart for many years?"

"Yeah," I replied with a nod. "He worked with my father, and we presumed them dead after a huge cave-in. They left me all alone. I…" My chin dropped to my chest, and I fussed with the hem of my shirt as my mind dredged up the painful memories. "I drowned my sorrows in alcohol. For way too long. I became dependent on it. And now, it's near impossible to resist it. I was doing good, though, before Horus kidnapped me. Then he—" I shook my head. I felt so pathetic. "He must have somehow picked up on my weakness."

"And you're sure he didn't just pull that information from your mind?"

"No, I'm sure," I said. "It's, uh, it's not hard to tell I crave it when it's in front of me. Nothing else matters."

We let a comfortable silence hang between us, matched by the stillness of the room. It felt good to be sharing my agony with someone. To talk about tragic events that brought me to this very moment in time.

I cleared my throat. "You know, I never thanked you for helping me with those two guards before."

Eirik brightened and took a seat on a bench carved of stone. "No thanks necessary, Andie. We're…friends, correct?" I nodded. "And your friendship is something I'm very grateful for. You're teaching me things about myself that I never knew before."

A tired laugh escaped my body. "Like the fact that you're basically an Amazonian warrior?"

Their eyebrow quirked, but they smiled through it. "If you're referring to my brute strength and agility, then yes. Among other things."

Suddenly, the door swung open and in walked the same woman that brought us here. She carried a wide copper tray of fruits and breads, a pitcher of wine balanced perfectly, and set it down on a table before wordlessly seeing herself out. The lock clicked again, and I eyed the tray. Not for the food, but for the liquid promise that beckoned me from the jug.

I licked my dry lips and stared into it as a sticky sweat broke out under my arms. My hands shook, wanting to desperately put the thing to my lips. If I could just take a few sips, take the edge off my rattled nerves, maybe I could think straight enough to figure a way out of this.

But, without a word, Eirik grabbed the clay pitcher and swiftly lunged for the window where they dumped the entire thing out. My heart squeezed, crying for the sweet red drink, but I quickly settled into a cloud of rationality.

"Thank you," I breathed.

"Have you told Silas of your struggle with this affliction?"

The corner of my mouth twitched at the use of his other name from someone other than me or Dad. It told me Eirik acknowledged Amun was a different man now, that they accepted the duality that he'd taken on and that he clearly preferred one side over the other. The side he'd built with me.

I shook my head and sat down. "No. I'm too ashamed."

Eirik walked over and peered down at me. "There's no shame to be had. We all deal with grief in different ways, some of us just need help to climb back out of it."

The door opened again and in shuffled a stumpy looking figure, their arms draped in fabrics of every kind. A measuring tape of some sort dangled around their neck. They turned, and I saw their face; an older woman with a pinched expression, years of life wrinkled into her skin. Her dark hair pulled back in a tight bun and held in place with a beautiful gold cuffing. A cerulean robe hung to the floor, covering her tiny body. She appeared human, but I wasn't entirely sure.

Shadow hissed at the stranger as she set down her things and came right for me. My average height towered over her by at least a foot and a half, and she reached up to maul my face.

"My, I wished they'd told me I'd be dressing such a beauty. Perhaps I would have brought finer garments." She pulled at my cheeks and raked fingers through my hair as she clucked her tongue.

Eirik intentionally cleared their throat. "I assume you won't have anything appropriate to dress me in?"

The woman craned her neck and eyed Eirik up and down. "Dear, I've been dressing kings and queens for years. And I've had a go at my fair share of beings from other worlds. All sorts of shapes and sizes. It may have been years since I've seen one, but I can dress a Venuvian before breakfast."

"So, you're aware of our modest culture?" Eirik challenged.

"Yes, yes," the woman replied impatiently and fussed with the heap of textiles she'd brought. "Mostly covered, light linens." She waved at the air between them. "I know." She pulled the ribbon from around her neck and held it close to her face, narrowing her beady eyes at the symbols along its length. "Let's get you both measured, shall we?"

I stood with my arms out as she sized me up with the measuring tape. Eirik sat waiting by the food tray and popped grapes in their mouth, one after another, while tossing a few for Shadow to catch in his toothy opening.

"Are you one of the many people under Horus' thumb?" I dared ask.

The woman chortled. "He wishes. I've been dressing the monarchs of this land for years. And I do it better than anyone else can. I was one of the few who traded with Star People before Horus banned them from the cities. I possess fabrics and materials from all over the universe." She pushed my legs apart and wrapped the tape around my upper thigh. "They reward me well for my services. Horus among them."

"I can see that." I wanted this woman to trust me. Perhaps I could convince her to leave the door unlocked when she left. It was a longshot, but I had to try. "Um, my name is Andie Godfrey, by the way."

Her brown beady eyes met mine, and she searched them. "Mera," she offered and, after a beat, turned to pluck some black netting from the pile and hung it across my body as she examined it with scrutiny.

"Mera," I said cautiously, trying to play it cool. "So, what's this event for, anyway?"

Eirik caught my line of sight from over the woman's back, and I discretely pleaded with a shake of my head for them to remain quiet.

"Lord Horus is throwing a party in honor of the king's

birthday. Everyone important will be in attendance, and the common folk will gather outside in the city square in celebration, too. It'll be quite the affair."

"So, my friend and I aren't really the partying type," I told her. She stopped rummaging through the fabrics and stood straight. "I was wondering if, maybe, you'd be so kind as to leave the door unlocked when you leave?"

She threw her head back in a raspy cackle of laughter. "Nice try. But I'm not just rewarded for my expert sewing ability, dearie. My loyalty also collects a pretty price."

My stomach clenched, and I exchanged a doomed look with Eirik.

Mera looped the tape over her neck again and scooped up the pile of fabrics she came in with. "I've got what I needed. I'll be back in a few hours with your outfits."

"A few hours?" I squawked. "What are we supposed to do in here for a *few hours*?"

The seamstress stopped in the doorway and half turned with a shrug of nonchalance. "You seem tightly wound. Perhaps a nap would do you some good."

She shut the door, and I waited for the click of the lock, hoping maybe she'd forget. But she didn't. I flew into pacing-mode and wiped the sheen of sweat from my forehead. I had to find a way out of here, one that would safely get Silas out with us.

"I wonder what ridiculous garb that wretched woman

will stick me in," Eirik spoke and lobbed off a chunk of bread. Shadow protested up at them from the floor and they tore off a piece to throw to him.

Something didn't sit right with me about the whole thing. Horus was a notorious narcissist. There was no way he'd throw a big birthday party for the king. To willingly give attention to someone else other than himself. A jittery breath of air pressed from my lungs.

I stopped and plunked my hands on my hips. "I think the real question is, what's Horus *really* up to with this party?"

CHAPTER NINE

I closed the door and turned to join Eirik and Shadow behind the guard that came to escort us to the party. Another winged man, different from the other two I'd met before. I considered making Shadow stay behind, but I needed him with me in case we stumbled upon an escape route.

Eirik was speaking to me, but all I could hear against their muffled noise was the sounds of my own rampant heart banging in my chest, thrumming in my ears. The fear of having to be around Horus again sent my nerves on the fritz. What if Silas was right? What if his brother just kills me, if given the chance? Or what if he truly finds a way into my mind?

I wasn't sure which was worse.

Eirik's hand touched my arm, ripping me from within my own chaotic brain, and the sound of the approaching party rushed in with the volume cranked. I shook my head and blinked at my friend.

"Are you alright?" they asked. "You haven't listened to a word I've said."

"Sorry," I replied. "Just nervous. When someone wants you dead, accepting an invitation to their party isn't exactly the best idea."

We emerged through a wide archway and the jam-packed courtyard faced us. People gathered in bunches; talking, drinking, enjoying the melody of a live musician that carried through the air. The person sat near the fountain in the center and played something that resembled a harp made of bone.

Tables littered the party, filled with food and drink, all leading toward the front where a tall young man stood by a throne-like chair. Joyfully chatting with those around him. He wore a pleated skirt and a striped nemes on his head. The markings of a traditional king.

"That must be Menakaure," I whispered in awe. To witness an Egyptian king in the flesh and blood…this was something archaeologists could only dream of. And here I was, literally living it.

I noticed that our guard had disappeared, leaving Eirik and I standing in the elevated opening, unsure what to do or where to go. Then, one by one, eyes around the room fell on us and gazed. Some even whispered to one another and pointed in our direction.

I leaned toward Eirik. "Why is everyone staring at us?"

A cheeky grin spread across their face. "While I know I'm simply a vision in this beautiful garment, and my kind aren't exactly welcome here, I believe they're looking at you, Andie."

My face pinched in confusion. "Huh? What? Why–"

I followed my friend's gaze down toward my outfit and gasped. I hadn't even paid attention while Mera was dressing us. My mind had wandered so far to thoughts of escape. While Eirik looked like an ethereal angel in a stunning sleek silken robe that draped over their body like liquid ice, I wore a black netted dress that snugged my shape and showed far more skin than I was comfortable with. Gold cuffs and thick braided straps of leather covered my bits, but I still felt naked. Exposed. I could feel heavy makeup tugging at the skin around my eye and I panicked.

"Jesus!" I wrapped my arms across my body. "I can't go in there like this!"

Eirik laughed and gently pried one of my arms away. "You look amazing, Andie." They shrugged. "Albeit, it's a far cry from the modest culture I'm accustomed to, but I can't deny that you look like something worthy of a queen. Perhaps," they couldn't stop a giggle from bubbling out, "we could use you as a mighty distraction while we make an escape."

"Shut up!" I hissed, but then fell into laughter with them. I rolled my eyes. "Let's get this over with. We need to find Silas and get the hell out of here."

Eirik's silver gaze raked over the crowd. "Shouldn't be too hard. He's already found you."

I trailed their line of sight that cut through the people and met Silas' widened stare. His jaw hung open; mossy eyes unblinking as I made my way through the swarms of guests. This was perfect. We could grab him right now and slip out under the cover of the party. No one would even notice. Then I realized as I got closer…he stood next to his brother, and my heart plummeted.

So much for a quick escape.

They were both dressed similarly. Double pleated kilts, bare chests that showed off their perfect soft muscles. Horus' dark curls kissed his shoulders while Silas' messy brown waves sat messily atop his head. I veered as far from Horus as I could and sidled up next to his brother.

"What on earth are you wearing?" Silas whispered in my ear.

Some part of me delighted in his discomfort over my outfit. "What do you mean? I'm sure you've seen women wear stuff like this before. Here, before you met me."

He shook his head. "I spent thousands of years in a

rock, remember? Women definitely wore nothing like…" he gestured up and down my dress, "*that.*"

"My, Andie," Horus chimed in with a slick purr in his tone. "If I'd known you cleaned up so well, perhaps I would have found you more comfortable accommodations during your previous stay." He raised his brow and gawked at my exposed body.

I glared at him. "*Accommodations*?" I spat. "You mean being locked in a cell and left for dead like an animal?"

The man heaved an indifferent shrug, as if my time spent here under his capture meant nothing. Like it was no big deal. But it was a nightmare I'd carry to my grave. Being in his presence made my skin crawl. He turned and plucked two glasses from a passing tray and handed them out to Eirik and I.

"Care for a drink?" The sound of his voice was simple and sincere, but his chilling stare bored into me with dubious intent. His eyes fell on my mouth. "To…wet your lips."

Half of me wanted to accept the glass just so I could throw it in his face. But the other half of me knew that if I held the wine in my hands, I didn't have the willpower to not drink it. Silas' arm wrapped around my lower back as Eirik leaned in front of me and plucked both glasses from Horus' fingers before placing them back on another passing tray.

"We'd be fools to accept anything from you," my friend said.

Horus tensed and grimaced at the nearness of Eirik, as if the audacity that they dared to speak to him repulsed him. Anger toiled in my gut and I grit my teeth, trying with all my might not to make a scene. But Silas slipped his fingers in between mine and gently tugged at my hand. He turned from his brother, nudging my shoulder.

"Let's dance," he said curtly, and swayed me away into the crowd.

The farther I got from Horus, the better I felt. The more I could calm my temper and wade through the fog that clouded my mind. I inhaled a deep, warm breath, let it fill my lungs, and peered up at the man in my arms.

"Your brother makes my blood boil." My hands wrapped around his neck and I played with the curls at the back of his head.

"He has that effect on people."

"So, what's really going on here?" I asked and discreetly searched around for the closest exit. But it didn't matter, Horus' stare never left his brother's back.

Silas' hand firmed against my lower spine, splaying his fingers through the sparse netting that covered my skin. "What's going on is that you're half naked and I can't take my eyes off you."

"Focus. I still haven't forgiven you for what you did."

"What?"

I rolled my eyes. "Coming back here after everything we went through to save you. What's happening in your head? What were you *thinking*?"

His expression turned solemn. "I was thinking about you. It's always you." He sighed. "Andie, when you're in the picture, nothing else matters. I gave myself back to my brother to *save* you."

"And ship me off back to the future, to *what*? Resume my life of misery without you?"

We spun and swayed to the music.

"At least you'd be alive."

"That wasn't living," I muttered under my breath and let my chin fall to my chest.

Silas slipped his hand under it and lifted my face to look into my eyes. "What's that supposed to mean?"

I opened my mouth to speak, to finally tell him about my dark days wasted away in my father's home with a bottle of vodka in my lap. But Horus appeared at our side, hands behind him as he rocked back on his heels in wait.

"What do *you* want?" I snapped.

He held out a hand, palm up. "I'd like to ask for this dance."

Silas' grip on my waist tightened, and he pulled me closer. "Not a chance."

Horus arched an eyebrow mockingly. "You dare challenge me, brother? Twice I one day?"

I could feel the stifled rage burning under Silas' skin. He practically vibrated with it. "Our deal was Andie's total safety."

The vile man feigned offence. "Of course. You have my word. Our new agreement binds me from harming her. Now," he pulled a chalice of wine from behind his back and handed it to Silas, "The king needs a drink."

I expected him to say no, to tell his brother to get lost. But Silas' arms hesitantly slid from my body and accepted the task.

"*Silas*," I practically whined and flashed him an incredulous look.

"I'll be right back," he replied and kissed my forehead before disappearing into the crowd.

My feet moved to run after him, but Horus yanked on my arm and spun me around where I collided against his chest. I squirmed in his grasp, but he refused to relent. The more I struggled, the closer he held me to him. He gripped my hip while his other hand forced fingers through mine, practically breaking my fingers, ready to dance. His hold tightened, squeezing my fingers and asserting dominance in the most subtle way. But I wasn't about to let him intimidate me. I squeezed back, cracking a few of his knuckles, and Horus' brow rose in surprise.

He chuckled and immersed us in the crowd as he spun

us around. "I like you," he noted. "You've got spite. I can relate to that."

"Don't waste your energy," I spat. "Because I despise *you*."

His chin rose proudly as his eyes scanned the room. I whipped my head around, trying to see what he was looking for.

"Give it time," he said. "I can be quite likeable."

I guffawed and pushed back when he tried to bring me closer, keeping at least a few inches between us. "I find that hard to believe."

He didn't reply, just kept prancing me around like nothing was wrong.

"You know," I added. "If you hate your brother so much, why keep him alive? Why toy with him like this?"

His dark gaze scrutinized me for a moment. "Destroying my brother is a harder task than one would think. I can kill his body, but his soul will always live in that damn amulet." He stopped and spun me around, then hauled me back to slam into his chest. He held me there, refusing to even allow me the room to wiggle. "Besides," his warm breath smoothed over my face, "Who says I hate Amun? I love my brother dearly, almost as much as I love myself. It is *he* who hates me."

"If you think that's true, then you're a fool," I replied as I shimmied my arm between us and pried some space there with my elbow. "Sil–Amun loves you more than you deserve. Why do you think he left his life behind to come here and save you from yourself? Why do you think he was willing to sacrifice the relationship he has with me, and send me away, just so he could stay here and appease *you*?"

Horus's embrace relaxed, as did his hard expression, and for a moment I witnessed a flash of something in his eyes. Innocence? Remorse? Something else? So fleeting, I would have missed it if I weren't looking right at him, because he quickly threw up the wall and hid behind a mask of jealousy.

He had no response and continued to dance us around the courtyard. Bypassing guests and onlookers as he vibrated with a heat that rattled me inside. It pissed him off, that much I could tell. Clearly, he didn't like the truth being shoved in his face. I felt his fingertips dig into the tender skin of my back and I winced. This man could end me in the blink of an eye.

I had to calm him.

I inhaled a nervous breath. "Delightful party. I bet you're just loving the attention." I attempted a light grin and hoped it was enough to rein him back.

Horus waited a beat and then let out a harrumph. "One would assume." He craned his neck and stared longingly toward the front where the king stood talking to Silas. "But tonight, the attention is not on me. No matter how much I wish it to be."

I shook my head. "I don't get it. If you can control people's minds, why don't you just use that power to make everyone love you?"

His brows rose, impressed. "It doesn't work that way. I need to be close to them, and as many as a city's worth is simply too much."

A coy grin twitched the corner of his mouth and he spun me around again as the music picked up. When he brought me back to his chest this time, his finger reached up to caress my cheek and I couldn't help but cringe away.

He leaned in, mouth touching my ear. "Besides, I have other ways of getting what I want."

I shoved at him, but it was useless. He was much stronger than me without even trying. "What is this, Horus?" I demanded. "Are you trying to prove to everyone, even the king, how you can control your brother? Because no one cares."

He threw his head back and laughed, a sound that unnerved my soul. He was clearly unhinged. In one swift move, his hand cupped the back of my head, twisting his fingers in my hair and tugging to the point of pain. But I refused to let out a sound, to give him the satisfaction of knowing he was hurting me. Slowly, he pushed my head toward him as he leaned into my face, his heaving breaths spilling over my skin. His mouth neared mine and panic shot through my veins, followed by a slight relief as he veered to the side and whispered in my ear.

"It's so much more than that."

A harsh shove sent me stumbling back, struggling to remain on my feet. I noticed how he stood calmly and faced the front where his brother was chatting with the king. Most of the crowd watched with him, admiring their ruler on his birthday. But something sinister lurked in the way Horus stood in wait. His hands together in front of him, chin held high with a smug grin.

I stared with them, watching, waiting for something to happen. Silas handed the king the chalice of wine and Menkaure accepted it graciously. He put it to his lips and drank, a long drawn out gulp, before raising it to the crowd. They all cheered and joined him in raising their own glasses.

Eirik appeared by my side. "What's going on?"

"I'm not sure–"

Suddenly, the king's hand shot to his throat, and he choked as his face filled with crimson. Silas, who still stood next to him, tried to help, but the man hit the floor like a rock. My heart pounded in my chest, a dose of panic coursing hot through my veins. Screams from the crowd pierced the air, and Horus' devious expression turned to look at me before he disappeared into the mass of frightened people.

"Oh my..." Eirik whispered in shock. "Horus...just poisoned the king."

My stare cut through the waves of guests and locked with Silas' panicked eyes. "And he made it look like his brother did it."

CHAPTER TEN

"Amun killed the king!" a woman shouted from the mass of crowd pushing around.

Chaos ensued in a matter of seconds. Fists flying, bodies stumbling to the floor. People rushed to the front of the party where their monarch lay dead on the stage, and Silas fought off those who were trying to detain him. He shoved someone down and then searched for me.

"Run!" I screamed at him. "I'll find you!"

But he wouldn't go. We worked our way toward one another while the panicked guests slammed into me, tossing me back and forth. I lost Eirik and Shadow in the disorder, but I knew they could handle themselves.

I could hardly move, the air was constantly knocked from my lungs as I got thrown about.

"Andie!" I heard Silas' cry.

"Just go!" I yelled, hoping he could hear me.

Eirik appeared and grabbed the few people near me and shoved them out of the way. They came to my side, breathy and tired, and put a protective arm around me.

"Go!" they shouted to Silas. "I've got her! Just run and hide!"

I caught sight of him through the people that zipped by, his angry and tortured expression. He didn't want to leave me any more than I wanted to leave him. But they trapped him on the elevated platform with a mob of pissed off worshipers who'd turned on their beloved Amun in the blink of an eye. He had to get away.

Two winged guards narrowed in on him, but Silas hauled back and punched his way through before leaping out an open window arch. A trembled gasp escaped my throat but Eirik held me in an assuring embrace.

"It's okay, he'll be fine," they told me. "It's a long way down, but Amun can do it with ease, I promise." They shoulder shoved another body out of the way. "No, let's go!"

It was just too much. The angry mob of guests were panicked or enraged and cared very little for those around them. Horus' guards struggled to keep order and safely usher everyone to the exit. But it was no use. A glass fell from somewhere and smashed at my feet, ricocheting off my bare legs and leaving tiny, painful gashes on my skin. I veered to the right, to go around the mess, but was knocked into a table and separated from Eirik once again.

I searched through anarchy for my friend, heaving breaths burning in my chest. Two hands reached out and grabbed my arms, spinning me around to face them. Horus. His fingers dug into my skin and I winced, but it only made him grip tighter.

His dark, crazed eyes drilled into me. "Never underestimate what I'm willing to do to get what I want."

He violently pulled me closer and put his mouth on mine in a kiss so painful it drew blood as my teeth tore the skin of my lips. A hefty and unexpected push threw me to the floor before he disappeared once more.

Unable to get to my feet, I cried out for help as legs trampled over me. Driving into my gut and kicking my face. My mouth filled with blood and I spat it on the floor while I fought for air. All the noise melded together, my mind spinning and sinking into hyperventilation. I curled into a ball in one last attempt to protect myself and, finally, two able hands hauled me to my feet.

"Eirik!" I said through sobs. The relief was palpable. "Can you get us to an exit?"

"Yes, I found the way we can go backward through the palace," they replied. "Follow me."

Shadow was there now with my bag in tow, our clothing

dragging from it. I scooped him up in my arms and we fought our way through the rising chaos until we found an empty, dark hallway. I had to stop and catch my breath.

"We're going to need to cover you," Eirik said. "You were seen dancing with Amun, and someone's bound to make the connection."

They pulled their old cloak from my bag and threw it over my shoulders. I stuffed my arms inside the too-long sleeves, grateful for the total coverage, and Eirik flipped the hood up over my head, shadowing my face.

"There we go," they said with a comforting smile, then their expression changed with concern. "Are you alright?"

I struggled to wade through the mess in my head, but I nodded. "I'm okay. W-we need to find Silas."

Eirik looked up and down the abandoned corridor we stood in. "It's doubtful he'll run directly back to the colony, for fear of being followed. But he can't be far."

I held Shadow in my arms and could feel his warmth seeping into my skin. He was scared and worried. We hurried through the palace and found an exit near the west side. The second we stepped onto the cool sand, sounds of more rioting came from the city square not far in the distance. We snugged the massive stone wall that surrounded Horus' home and sneaked out into the city where we were met with even larger crowds of chaos. People yelled, chanted, cheered. Fires billowed from piles of what looked like garbage. We kept our distance, careful not to bring any attention our way.

"Jesus, this didn't take long," I said.

"Menkaure was loved deeply," Eirik replied. "Even with Horus dictating his every move."

"It doesn't make any sense." I cuddled Shadow. "Why kill a king you already control?"

"I'm not certain." They tugged at my sleeve to veer us away from an approaching guard. "My only concern right now is getting us out of here safely."

Just then, the volume of nearby rioters increased, and I turned around to find a group of men hauling on ropes tied around a giant flaming monolith. I squinted to make out the symbols and realized it was a monument dedicated to the worship of Amun. It towered overhead and slowly moved, leaning to one side.

And headed right for us.

Someone grabbed me from behind as Eirik pushed and I stumbled into the cover of trees where Silas secured me in his grasp. I let go of Shadow and he scampered over to Eirik while I flung my arms around my savior's neck.

"Oh my God, I thought you were dead," I said with a tremble in my voice. I kissed his mouth, over and over and mauled his face in my hands.

Silas kissed me back, his sweaty muscles tensing in desperation. "We have to get back to the colony before we're followed."

"Yes, we should get moving," Eirik urged.

"Amun!" someone shouted from the crowd. I whipped my head to the side to find people pointing right at us in the treeline. "Amun is there!"

"Murderer! Make him pay! Kill him!" The sounds of violent cries hit us like a wave as the crowd moved like one being, making their way toward us.

Silas spun in my arms. "Go."

I shook my head frantically. "No, not without you! Just come with us!"

He broke free of our embrace and looked to Eirik. "Take her into the forest, as far away as possible."

They nodded dutifully. "Of course."

"What? No!" I protested. "Silas, just come with us!"

His chest heaved. "Just trust me. Please."

I didn't have any fight left in me and watched with tear-filled eyes as he turned to face the oncoming mass. Eirik continued to pull me along, taking me farther into the forest as instructed. I tripped over roots and rocks, struggling to keep my footing while watching for Silas.

Eirik picked up speed. "We have to get as far as we-"

Suddenly, a blast of energy cut through the air, booming in my ears and tossing me from my feet. Eirik slammed into a tree and I landed on the ground where I skidded across the dirt. My ears thrummed as if a bomb had gone off. In the distance, the disjointed sound of bodies–so many bodies–hitting the sand made my stomach roll.

Shakily, I pushed up from the ground. "What the hell was that?"

Eirik fumbled to their feet and scooped up Shadow in one arm while hauling me up on wobbly legs. Their silver stare fixed on me.

"Just one example of the substantial power Amun possesses." They pulled my hood back up over my head. "It should have bought him time to get away. Now, come on!"

Without a word, I obeyed my friend and followed them through the darkness, plunging deeper and deeper into the cover of forest. But with every step I took, I put more distance between me and Silas. With every passing second, my mind raced to justify what had just happened. What did he do? Where did that blast of energy come from? It was as if a small bomb went off. My heart ached, unable to reconcile with the drastic turn of events that just unfolded before my very eyes. I was pretty sure Horus didn't want me dead, but now I worried for the life of the man I loved.

CHAPTER ELEVEN

I couldn't stand it anymore. I had to sit up. The lumpy rocks of the cave floor that had jabbed my side all night left me feeling bruised and defeated. I hadn't slept for a single second. Not that I expected much from a dirty, wet cave in the middle of nowhere. But there were other things that kept me staring into the darkness. Like the impending doom that constantly hovered overhead. What would Horus do next? Would he ever stop? Would he leave his brother alone? How long could I survive in this time when a God of Vengeance didn't know whether to use me or kill me?

The tease of early morning sun crept inside the small cavern we'd taken refuge in the night before. That wretched black netted dress sat in scraps a few feet away, and I hugged my knees to my chest from inside Eirik's old cloak as I stared at it in the floor. Last night was one I'll never forget. I'd played out the entire sequence of events as I lay on the cave floor for hours, and I still couldn't reconcile any of it. The whole thing felt like a vivid dream stuck on repeat in my short-term memory.

From behind me, Shadow stirred and Eirik moaned as they rolled over. I half turned and looked at them.

"Morning," I muttered.

Eirik sat up and stretched their long arms in the air. "Did you sleep well?"

I closed my eyes. "I'm not even going to dignify that with an answer."

They waited a beat. "That's fair."

Shadow crawled into my lap and put his hand to my neck, releasing that familiar warmth.

"He wants to go home," I said.

"It should be clear," Eirik replied. "Any of Horus' men who may have been searching for us would surely be gone by now."

"Good." I painfully rose to my feet. "Let's go."

But if I were being honest, I didn't worry about us. All my thoughts became consumed with whether Silas was alive and made it back to the colony.

I guess we'd soon find out either way.

***

Eirik made a beeline for their medical supplies to treat my wounds, while I sped off to my father's quarters. Exhaustion pulled at my every muscle, threatening to drag me down, but pure adrenaline fueled my steps. We'd made it back in one piece. I just hoped I could say the same for Silas.

I cut through the Great Hall, just in case he was there. Breakfast had just finished and most of the colonists had cleared out. All except a few that lingered, Anubis among them. When he spotted me storm into the room, he shot up from his chair as his jackal form melted away and Niya appeared at his feet, trotting alongside him.

He met me in the middle. "Andie! Where have you been? What's going on? We just got word of rioting that happened in the city."

I sucked in a deep breath, stomping down the rising grief that formed in my gut. *He didn't make it back.* Anubis' questions affirmed it. With one hand on my hip and the other bracing my sweaty forehead, I paced the few feet in front of him as Eirik's too-long cloak dragged on the floor.

"Andie…" Anubis stepped closer, hesitant and worried. "Your father's been worried sick. What's happening? Are you alright?"

"No," the word spattered over my bottom lip. Tears

swelled in my eyes. "I don't know what…it's all messed up. I can't…"

"Sit down." He ushered me over to a chair. "Just breathe."

"Did Silas come back here?" I asked.

He slowly shook his head, his expression waiting. "No. I thought he was with his brother?"

"Eirik and I snuck to Horus' palace yesterday to get him out," I told him and tried to ignore the immediate look of disapproval. "We expected to find him locked up somewhere, like…" I swallowed nervously, "Like I was. But Silas was just strolling around the place like it was any ordinary day. His brother caught us, then made us attend this stupid party for the king."

"Your father said you left, but we'd no idea you actually went to the palace." Anubis's wide eyes stared at me, trying to keep up. "Is that when you got separated?"

I shook my head. "No, that's when Horus poisoned the king and framed Silas in front of half the city. I didn't even have time to blink before the rioting broke out."

He leaned back in his chair and nodded slowly. "Hence the destruction we heard about."

I rocked back and wrapped my arms tight around my torso. "We barely made it out alive. Eirik and I ran for a cave. Silas stayed behind to deal with a mob. He used some kind of…" I really fought to work through that detail in my mind. "There was this blast of energy."

Anubis nodded knowingly. "He would have gotten away, then."

"Where would he go if not here?" I asked.

He thought for a moment as he absently reached down to pet an affectionate Niya. His stare turned blank as he drifted off, thinking. "He wouldn't go to his mother's. That's the first place Horus would look. And he wouldn't dare stay in the city." Anubis looked at me from across the table. "He'd come here. I know he would. But he'd stay away for a while, to lose any followers."

I rubbed my hands over my face and willed myself to calm. "Yeah, that's what Eirik and I did. Found a cave for the night."

"He would have done the same. And he won't use the main entrance."

"What do you mean?" But then I realized. He'd take a less risky way. A front. I lit up with the idea. "Osiris' temple on the other side of the colony."

Anubis stood up, and I shot to my feet. "You go to the temple. I'll head to your father's and fill him in on everything that's happened."

I nodded once and dutifully before bounding off toward the temple that Osiris built as a hidden entrance to the colony. It was the perfect cover, and I suddenly felt bad for not thinking of using it when Eirik and I returned. But

I was so desperate to get inside. To safety. To Silas.

Now I sped down the winding stone corridors, still hoping to find him. My labored breaths echoed off the empty walls, matched by my every step. I finally reached the false wall and maneuvered the golden tablet embed there until the mass of stone rumbled and slid out of the way. He had to be here. He just *had* to be.

But the place was bare.

I peeked out from around a wide column, cautiously scanned for any sign of movement. Carefully, I moved further into the temple, keeping to the shadows as I checked different chambers. The wide entrance came into view and a fresh breeze caressed my face, tickling the skin with my hair.

My back snugged the wall as I crept closer, but I stopped in my tracks. Something moved outside on the ground. A shadow. Could it be Silas? Or maybe it was a guard. Or worse, Horus' looming shadow as he paced the skies. I waited for more movement, for something—*or someone*—to emerge, but nothing happened. My heart raced so fast it made me nauseous, and I closed my eyes as I fought to breathe through the wave.

Nervously, I approached the doorless entry and inched around the mouth of the temple to peer outside just as a figure clamoured inside and nearly knocked me off my feet. A scream escaped from me, my body shoved up against a wall, and a dirty hand cupped my mouth. But all fear washed away as I peered up into the wild eyes of the man I loved.

I pulled down on his hand and desperately put my lips to his, raking my fingers through the back of his hair as his entire body leaned against me. I severed our kiss, and we both heaved for air, our foreheads pressed together.

"Are you alright?" I asked.

"Yes," he replied. "I took cover under an uprooted tree for the night. Horus and his men circled the skies for hours, but they never came down to the ground." Silas leaned back and examined me. "Are you okay?"

"Yeah, Eirik and I slept in a cave. We just got back." I rolled up the frumpy sleeves of the cloak I still wore, noting how dirt and moss stains covered his half naked body. "How–what was that last night? That thing you did in the city square."

"It's…one of my abilities," he said, uncertainty in his tone. Was he afraid to tell me?

"What does that mean?"

Silas' shoulders slumped. "I can manipulate the elements around me with energy. As if–it's like I'm connected to the universe in a way no one in my family is. Perhaps, because I was *made* rather than born." He waited a moment, allowing me time to let it sink in. He searched my face with a sense of desperation. "But no matter how powerful I am, it'll still never be enough to protect you from all the dangers of this world. Of this *time*. It's not safe for you here."

Then I remembered what he'd done and shook away the fog of relief as I shoved at his chest like a scorned child. "I'm still pissed at you!" I told him, failing to ignore the sheer look of betrayal wrought across his face.

"What?" His forehead pinched together.

"For going back to your brother," I told him angrily. "For trying to ship me back to the future. *Without* you! Without even a goodbye."

"Andie, I've always done things your way. Always. Now it's time we do this one thing my way. I can't stop my brother if I have to worry about your life, too."

I shook my head, fighting back tears of frustration as I turned to storm away. But Silas caught my arm and pulled me back.

"I promise to come back to you once I'm done what I need to do." His jeweled stare pleaded for me to understand.

I let the tears spill over. "How can you ask me to just turn my back and leave you?"

He sighed impatiently. "I'm not…asking."

I don't know what came over me. Years of unresolved heartache, the effects of recent events, the rollercoaster of life and death that constantly hauled me along like a ragdoll. Who knew? But something—a breaking point, perhaps—clicked in my mind and I hauled back before slapping his face so hard my hand immediately stung from the impact.

"You don't get to decide," I said steadily.

Silas rubbed his cheek, but there was no look of retaliation on his face. He knew he deserved it. Still, a ping of regret touched my heart and seeped out.

I chewed at my lip, trying to bite back the wave of tears. "I'm sorry."

"It's okay," he assured me solemnly. "Bound to happen eventually."

"I can handle myself, you know," I kept my even tone. "You don't have to worry about me."

"But I *will*. I do, all the time. Nothing else in this world is as important to me as your life, Andie."

"Exactly." I jabbed a finger at his shoulder. "My life. I choose what's done with it. I choose to stay. I choose to fight to be with you. Silas," I slowly neared, "you don't have to do this alone."

He fixed his stare on the floor. Distant. Calculating. Then he sprung to life and grabbed my upper arms, pushing me up against the hard wall with a smack that nearly knocked the breath from my lungs. But it wasn't an act of anger, but one of desperate passion. His mouth was on me and all thoughts of worry or anger fled from my mind.

My hands clawed at his shoulders, frantic and anxious, pulling him as close as I could. His weight leaned against me as his torso rolled, hot and wanting. One hand feverishly worked to rip the tattered cloak from my body, leaving me exposed as he hoisted me up. My weak legs wrapped around his naked waist and the pressure of his driving thrust forced a loud cry of pleasure from me. Silas stifled the sound with his mouth over mine, devouring my lips in a breathy kiss.

"God, I love you," the words heaved from my throat.

Silas' fingers curled in my hair and tugged, forcing my face to tip upward. His cheek, warm and pulsing, smoothed against mine as his words tickled my ear. "I love you, too."

I remained nailed to the wall by his able body, my legs wrapped tight around him like a vice. His mossy eyes searched mine for an answer to the question that sparkled in his gaze, and I nodded.

A part of me, the part I could never trust, the addict, needed Silas now more than I ever have. Like a drink, he was the elixir of my salvation. I just wished he'd stop trying to send me away, right back into the waiting arms of my addiction.

And just like that, I knew I could no longer keep it a secret from him. I had to tell Silas how I let alcohol ruin my life after he disappeared. But that was a conversation for later. Right now, all I wanted was to drink him in, to get lost in the God of a man that held my heart in his capable hands.

And so I did.

CHAPTER TWELVE

If I were staying in the past, then we couldn't let the key to time travel fall into the wrong hands. The portal must be deactivated. But it wasn't a choice that was totally mine to make.

Silas walked with me, hand in hand, toward my father's quarters. We'd slipped back to my room first so I could get some regular clothes, but the skin of my back still stung from the scratchy wall of Osiris' temple. I grinned and touched my finger to my tender lips. It was a welcome pain.

Silas knocked at the old wooden door and we waited a moment until the sound of footsteps shuffling across the dirt floor could be heard. The door swung open and Dad's eyes widened at the sight of us.

He immediately took me in his arms. "Peach, you're

alright. You had me worried sick."

"I'm sorry," I told him, then tossed a sarcastic nod toward Silas. "But someone had to go save this idiot."

Dad, confused, smiled through it and patted Silas on the arm. "It's good to see you well and alive, my friend."

"I'm not sure she'd have it any other way," Silas replied.

Dad chuckled and turned back in the doorway. "Come in, come in. I assume we have things to discuss."

Anubis was inside, sitting at the little table with Niya curled at his feet. "I see we thought correctly."

"Yeah," I replied and plunked down on the lumpy mattress. My body relented to exhaustion and I desperately wanted to fall into a coma. But my mind was alive with thoughts of everything that lay ahead. "You were right. Didn't take long for him to show up."

"So," my father chimed in as he stirred a bubbling pot over the little open fire pit nestled in the wall. "Explain what's going on in the city. Should we be concerned?"

Silas and I exchanged a look. "Yes, very concerned. Horus hosted a massive party for the king's birthday. Then had Silas serve him poisoned wine. He fell to the floor, dying instantly in front of half the city."

Dad's furrowed brow caught the light of the fire. "Why on earth would he do that? He controls the king."

"I guess to mar Silas' reputation with the people?" I suggested. "It's all I can think of." I glanced at Silas who stood leaned against the wall by the door. "He behaves like a selfish child. He does these things because he wants attention. Your attention. He wants to be loved and thinks you don't care about him."

He raked his fingers through his hair and lowered to a squat. "No matter what I do to prove him wrong, he'll never believe that he can earn love. He'll always think he has to take it."

"And we all know he'll do anything to attain it," Anubis added.

"Which is why we must protect the portal now more than ever," I said. Dad quirked his head, curious. "Horus can't get inside my mind, not yet anyway. But if he ever finds a way, if he ever got his hands on *you*…it's not enough to just protect it. It has to be deactivated."

"What do you mean?" Dad questioned. "Destroy our only ticket home?"

I shrugged helplessly. "Is that not what you were willing to do before? When Silas ordered you to take me back to the future?" The second my words touched the air, I gasped and whipped my head toward Anubis with a fright.

Silas stepped forward, a reassuring hand held out toward me. "It's okay, I already told him everything."

I let out a heavy sigh of relief. It'd be nice not to have to watch my every word around him. Anubis just nodded in understanding, then stood from his seat.

"Horus has spent years trying to track down this portal, to use it to travel to our hidden mother site on the other side of the world. He wants to get off planet to find one he can rule himself." Anubis eyed us all intently. "But if he *ever* found out that the portal we protect can now send people through time…there's no telling what he could do with that. He could go back to when we first arrived on this plant and eradicate all Star People. Claim this world for himself."

I scooted off the bed and walked over to my father. "I've made my decision. I'm staying here with Silas. There's nothing left for me back in the future." I took his hand in mine, a hand that had guided me for so long. "But you have a choice, though. You can go home where it's safe before we destroy the portal key."

Dad regarded me with a look of disbelief, and the needy part of my soul desperately hoped he stayed. I was too selfish to make him go, no matter how much I knew it was the right thing for him to do.

"Andelyn," he spoke with a soothing tone that reached the child in me. "You're my flesh and blood. My only child, my only tie to this world. Do you honestly think I'd ever willingly choose to leave you? To live in a world where you didn't exist?" The wrinkles around his eyes scrunched together. "How can I go back knowing what I know? And like you said before, I could never explain my sudden reappearance. I'm staying with you." He squeezed my hand and tears stung my dry eyes. "I'm *never* leaving you behind again."

"Then it's settled," I said, and turned to face the gods in the room. "Let's go deactivate a portal."

***

I held my breath as we descended the stone staircase that lowered us into the pit. Images flashed across my vision; the struggle with Howard on the landing, the knife in the gut, the impact when my dying body smacked against the floor below.

My feet touched the bottom and I let my lungs deflate. I suddenly felt cold, but I knew it was just the residue of fear in my veins. Silas and Dad made their way toward the middle, where I'd once fallen. The portal.

"Are you okay?" Anubis asked.

I shivered. "Yeah, just strange standing in the exact spot where I died."

"You didn't die," he replied firmly.

I pursed my lips as I slowly nodded. *Didn't I, though?*

Everything I am, my entire existence, was gone. Left behind in a time I'll never return to. The entire world, the only one I knew, considered me dead. And, in some ways, I was. Passed on, moved on, whatever you wish to call it. I was *here* now, living a new life. Who's to say that's not what we do when we die?

Silas stood in the center, over the keystone, while Dad held a new one to replace it. I couldn't get close; the wicked memory of what Howard did was still too fresh. I wasn't sure I'd ever get over it. So, I held back a few feet and did my best to hold it together.

Apparently, my best wasn't enough.

Anubis said nothing, but he discreetly took my hand and stood with me in solidarity. My pulse slowed and I could fill my lungs without the weight of fear beating down on them. In that moment, I realized I was making connections here. More than I ever had in my entire life. Like with Eirik and Shadow. It was a new sensation, but some strange part of my soul wanted more of it. I never really knew much about Silas' past or his family before. And now, here, I could see the people who've shaped him. Anubis, his mother, even his wretched brother. I suddenly felt more connected to him than ever before.

We watched in silence as Silas stood and reached his hand into the air. His foot stomped the floor and a glorious staff shot up from below. The same one that he once used to…kill me. He caught it in a stern grip and its tip–a golden sphere–glowed like sunshine. I had to shield my eyes with my hand.

He raised it up, every muscle in his body tensing as he

brought the point of the staff down on the stone with an ear-piercing clang. I flinched and covered my ears as the sound echoed off the cavern with nowhere to release. The air vibrated long after the sound dissipated. Silas set down his staff and knelt to pull the shattered bits of stone from its slot while Dad clumsily dropped the new blank one in place.

And just like that, time travel was no more.

They filled their arms with the broken pieces and came over to where we stood in wait. I still couldn't believe it. Yes, I made the choice to stay, but now the possibility of returning home was truly gone. It was just an idea before now, and the finality of it stirred dizzily in my mind, searching for a place to settle.

"How're you doing, Peach?" Dad asked and struggled with the heavy bits of stone. "Being down here, after what Howard did."

I shrugged, not wanting my father to worry, as Anubis took one of the larger pieces off his hands. "I'm fine."

He kissed the top of my head and then turned to follow Anubis up the stairs. I moved to trail behind, but Silas tugged at my sleeve and held me back.

His eyebrows rose with widened eyes. "Are you, though?"

"What?"

"Are you okay?" he continued. "You've been through

a great deal these last few days, even more so since you traveled through the portal."

My nostrils flared as I sucked in a deep breath. I was tired of being afraid, tired of being in pain, sick of yielding to my demons. So, I took a moment to admire his raw beauty, the sharp line of his worried mouth, traced my thumb under the skin of eye and cupped his cheek.

"I'm good," I told him with as much certainty as I could muster. "I'm with you."

Silas' hand moved up to cover mine on his face and he kissed my palm. His soft green eyes flashed with an idea and he grinned. "Well, if you're going to be sticking around and constantly throwing yourself in peril, then you're going to need a backup plan."

"What do you mean?"

He hugged me close with a tired but hopeful sigh. "Let's go see my mother."

CHAPTER THIRTEEN

We strolled across the cool marble floors of Isis' mansion while in search of her. Silas still had yet to tell me what we were doing here, and being in a place where Horus could so easily find us made me jittery inside.

My head whipped back and forth, scanning every line. Every shadow.

"Are you going to tell me what's going on or are you just planning to let me die of an anxiety attack?"

To my side, he snickered and took my hand as he led me to his mother with a total confidence of exactly where she was in the building.

"Just wait," Silas teased.

We turned a corner and emerged into a luscious garden.

The ceiling opened up to the sky, sunshine beamed down, nourishing the vivid colors of plant life. Flowers of all sorts; white Egyptian lilies, pink lotus, the scent of jasmine heavy in the air.

And there she was. Isis.

As always, she was radiance. Thin white fabric draped down her tall body, her dark golden hair gleaming in the sunlight, like copper. She caught sight of us in the corner of her eye and released a flower she'd been smelling from a low hanging vine.

"Silas!" she exclaimed and bounded for us. She smiled at me. "Andie."

"We've come to ask for your help," he jumped right to the chase. "Sorry for the curtness, but we're in a hurry."

"What's the matter?" she replied, her tone suddenly heavy with concern. "Does this have anything to do with what I heard? What on *earth* is happening in the city?"

He glanced at me and we shared a mutual sigh. Silas tipped his head. "Horus."

Isis gave a look of dismay only a mother could pull off and shook her lowered head.

I wrapped my arms across my body. "He's got some elaborate plan to make everyone hate…Amun. So, he can step in and act as the better brother…or *something*? The better God?" A groan rumbled in my throat. "We're not really sure."

The air became tight with her contrite silence. With a deep sigh, she spun on her heel and marched over to a small table that displayed various fruits and breads and poured herself a glass of wine. "That boy will never learn, will he?"

"Probably not," Silas agreed. "Which is part of the reason I came to you today. To ask your help."

Isis brightened. "Of course. What can I do?"

He hesitated. "Can you…create a soul stone for anyone?"

She searched his face cautiously and swirled her glass before taking a quick sip. "Theoretically, I can. But for whom?"

Silas turned to me and paled. Why was he nervous? Then I realized…

"For *me*?"

He nodded slowly. "If you want it."

My mind blanked. "Won't that mean I'll be…immortal?"

He exchanged a silent glance with his mother and then shrugged. "Yes. You'll essentially live forever, unless your amulet is destroyed." He waited and, when I didn't reply, he added, "Is that something you'd want to do? I mean, it's a decision of mass proportions."

I gawked at him. "The *biggest* proportions."

But a stifled chuckle burped from my chest and I

grinned. He worried I wouldn't want to be with him forever. I had no idea why I hesitated. While most would search for reasons why, I simply couldn't think of a single reason I *wouldn't*.

Freaked, but elated, I smiled, and it immediately eased the look on his face. "Be with you forever? It's not even a question."

Our chests heaved toward one another, pushed along by the high of the moment. But Isis cleared her throat and my stomach clenched as I looked at her bashfully.

"I said theoretically," she reminded. "I can't just create a soul stone out of nothing. She's a mere mortal." Isis gave me an apologetic tip of the head. "I'd need part of an immortal soul in order to create it."

"Take mine," Silas blurted.

My head whipped in his direction and a cool sweat broke out across my skin. "No! What?" I shook my head and stepped toward him, my palm sliding over his shoulder. "You can't just give me something like that."

His chin rose toward his mother. "Would it hurt me?"

She smiled proudly. "No, it wouldn't. I'd only need a sliver." She pinched together her thumb and index finger. "A minute grain."

Silas rubbed my upper arms, soothing me into the idea. "There. You see? Let me do this for you, Andie. For… myself. I can't stand the idea that you could die in so many ways here. All because you stayed for me. So," he puffed out a sigh, "I want to give you every fighting chance to survive."

I gave it half a second of thought as my face stretched tight with a grin. "Let's do it."

Isis nodded once and with finality as her cup clanged against the table where she placed it. "Very well then." She stepped back and widened her stance. "Bear with me, it's been a few millennia since I've done this."

I had no choice but to stand there and stare in awe as the Goddess closed her eyes and tensed her arms out at her sides. She was a sight to revere. The air seemed to cool, the sunshine dimmed, and a strange echo carried through the sudden breeze that tickled the air.

Tiny shimmering particles of dust began twirling around her, appearing from nowhere. Her hands moved slowly and with care as she pulled the specks into her palm. Against the warm brown of her skin, the small pile of dust glowed like moonlight.

"Stardust," Isis spoke, and I realized my mouth was hanging open. She grabbed a clay bowl from the table and carefully poured the bits from her hand. "The life force of the universe. Never dying, always reborn in another."

I shook the fog from my mind, breaking the captivating hold her very presence put on me. "It's just–" I looked at a beaming Silas. "I can't believe I get to see this. To experience these things. It's like a dream."

His fingers slipped in between mine, fingers of a hand I'd soon hold for the rest of eternity, and part of me danced inside at the thought.

Isis set the bowl down and looked at her son. "Now, for the next step. Are you ready?"

Silas nodded without missing a beat and released my hand. I stepped back a few paces, leery of witnessing part of someone's soul being sliced from their body. Would it be bloody? Quick? Would he feel it?

Her fingers stretched toward him, pinching the air in front of his chest as if she were coaxing an invisible strand of hair. Silas' entire body clenched and his back arched, but he made no sound of pain. The breath seemed to solidify in his chest, his eyes unblinking as they fixed on his mother. She continued to pluck at the air just an inch over his heart and, suddenly, her thumb and index finger withdrew a silver thread. It pulsed with life and wriggled in her pinched fingers.

"Holy sweet Jesus," I whispered and capped a hand over my mouth. I didn't know what to expect. This was the stuff of sci-fi movies. But to see a piece of Silas' soul like that, to witness its ethereal beauty, the magnitude of his sacrifice was that much more.

He slacked and leaned against an ivy-covered trellis. Instinctively, I went to him, but he waved me off. "I'm fine.

Just a little tired." He motioned toward his mother. "Just wait. She's not done."

My lips pursed as I backed away, giving him room to breathe and recoup the permanent energy just taken from him. Isis scooped up the clay bowl and let the luminous thread spool inside as she swirled it slowly with both hands, mixing the two eternal ingredients together. A pure white glow emanated upward and cast her patient face in starlight. I stared until my eyes watered over. I dared not blink, not wanting to miss a single second of this momentous ritual.

She came for me then. Her light steps making no sound as she neared. "The last ingredient is a drop of your blood." She held out her upturned palm in wait. "May I?"

As if in a trance, I slowly placed my hand in hers and immediately relished in the way it felt. Silky smooth, warm, comforting. Like a mother's embrace. Historically, Isis was the embodiment of motherhood and cared for all beings equally. People coveted her love for thousands of years. And the goddess held *my* hand. My heart strained with excitement and I breathed through the wave of adrenaline that desperately wanted to burst from my body.

Her perfect fingernail pierced the skin of my palm and she squeezed to draw blood to the surface. I let her turn it over, allowing red droplets to fall into the bowl where they instantly fused with the other ingredients. The bright white light pulsed and morphed with a tinge of crimson as she emptied the contents into her one hand before setting the bowl down and then cupping the enchanting pile with her other.

Her elbows stuck out as she pressed down, causing a strange and unsettling vibration to emanate outward. Light diffused with red seeped out from the cracks of her clenched hands and we all waited in awed silence until the glow dissipated and Isis finally pried open her grasp to reveal a single ruby the size of a large bottle cap.

"Is that it?" I asked, unable to take my eyes off the gem. "Is that…my soul stone?"

Silas was by my side, the warmth of his skin radiating through my clothes. Isis held out the ruby for me to take.

"It certainly is," she replied. "Keep it safe, tell no one whom you wouldn't trust with your own life, and–" Suddenly, her eyes flashed over our shoulders. "Anubis."

I spun around to find Silas' cousin striding toward us with purpose wrought in his worried expression. He wore his jackal form and a new black leather vest over his heaving chest.

"I have news," he said, and stopped in our little circle. "I'm not sure why I didn't realize it before, when Andie told me about what happened to the king."

"What do you mean?" I asked, anticipation beating wildly in my chest.

One of his pointed ears twitched. "Every soul that passes through to the Underworld, passes through me first. The king, his soul, he…never crossed over. He's not dead."

Silas paced. "So, it was all a trick then. A rouse?"

I shook my head, trying to wrap my mind around it all. "But why?"

"I'm not sure," Anubis replied thoughtfully. "But I also got word that Horus is in the city square eliciting riots and ramping up the people. He's saying that the God of Chaos and Destruction is upon them for the actions they've done in the king's death."

Silas fell ominously quiet and stepped back to comb stressed fingers through his hair.

"Set?" I said. "Your father? He's coming?"

Isis tensed. "No, it's impossible. Set is buried in a temple deep in the desert where no one can find him."

Her son cleared his throat nervously and ran his hand over his gaped mouth, a deep worry seeded in his mossy stare. "Well, that may not be entirely true. What if I told you Horus might know where that temple is?"

Isis, panicked, shook her head. "No, he couldn't…"

"In the palace the other day, before Andie showed up with Eirik, I overheard him discussing the idea of releasing our uncle, to bring him back." His gaze turned distant at the memory. "I didn't think he was serious. But now that I think of it, he was standing over a desk covered in maps and books. As if he'd been doing research."

My pulse quickened. "Yes, I've seen that room. That's how Eirik and I got in the palace, through the window."

"Well, if that's true," Isis said, all color drained from her beautiful face as she scooped up her glass of wine and downed the rest of it, "then I'd say we're all doomed."

CHAPTER FOURTEEN

Three of us sat around a table topped with a thick slab of dark wood. The intricate grains hypnotized me, luring me into the ease of its simple beauty. Like a marble cake. Isis fussed with filling its surface with plates of food and drink. She hadn't muttered another word since Anubis came and broke the news of what Horus has been up to.

"I just don't get it," Silas said. "Why *pretend* to kill the king?"

Anubis leaned his chair back on two legs and balanced it with ease as his expression remained staid. "I'm not sure. We're definitely missing something. Some kind of detail that puts it all together."

I shrugged and picked at a plate of grapes that Isis

shoved in front of me. "I'm more concerned with why he's drumming up all this chaos if he's just scolding the people for their actions. Warning them of Set's return." I paused and popped a grape in my mouth, shoving it to the side. "I mean, it's like taunting a beast and then getting mad when it retaliates."

"For the sake of anarchy?" Silas suggested without confidence. He shook his head. "And then intentionally releasing Set to make it even worse? He must know the consequences of bringing our uncle back. This fragile world won't survive Set's wrath."

Isis slammed down a silver tray of utensils, tears skimming her wide stare. "No."

"No?" Silas reiterated and then stood up from his chair to walk around the table to her. "Mother, we don't want this to be true any more than you do, but Horus is clearly up to something. If he really does release–"

"No!" she spoke again, but this time with angry desperation. She put her hands on the table and leaned forward on them. "It's impossible. After Set…dismembered your father, I used almost everything I had in my power to do the same to him. I forced him into his elemental form of sand and bound his body in two separate locations across the desert. Then I took a single grain of the sand and secured it in an abandoned temple before I destroyed it. Buried. Hidden. *Never* to be found."

The three of us looked to one another with uncertainty. This was obviously a topic Isis preferred not to discuss. And, until now, I never really thought about how it must affect her. Osiris, her one true love, father of her two sons, was killed–an act deemed impossible–by his own brother. She's been alone ever since. My heart ached for her because I knew exactly how she must have felt. For two years, I shared that same loneliness. I'd thought I'd lost my father and the man I loved to a cave-in and I had never wanted to face it.

Set was her Egyptian pit on the other side of the world.

Silas stroked her arm and eased her down into a chair. "Is it at all possible that Horus could have figured out where this temple is buried? Any way that he could have gotten his hands on the information?"

Her tawny waves shook. "I've never told a soul, never recorded it anywhere." She tapped the side of her head. "It's just been in here all this time and Horus has never penetrated my mind."

Anubis shoved off from his seat. "Well, whether or not we wish to believe it, Horus has some sliver of information that will lead him to find my father's resting place. His extreme actions these last few days say enough."

"If it's true," Isis entertained, "then he has no idea the mistake he's about to make. Set is an elder god. Only another elder god can possess the strength to defeat him.

With Osiris gone all these years, and the energy I spent to bind Set in the first place, I'm just…" She shook her head. "I worry I'm not strong enough."

I swallowed nervously. I didn't feel like I had a right to be in on this conversation. I mean, what could I possibly offer of value?

"What would happen?" I asked and all six eyes fell on me. "If Set were to escape. Would he really cause that much trouble?"

Isis poured herself another drink. "How would you feel if you were separated from the one being you loved, turned to sand, and then banished for thousands of years to live out eternity in a temple underground?" She drank long and desperate. "You'd be upset, to say the least. But the God of Chaos and Destruction might very well destroy the world as we know it."

I sank back in my chair. "So, that's a yes, then."

They continued discussing the contingencies and bantering about plans to thwart all possibilities. But everything circled back to one conclusion. A question. Why would Horus release Set knowing that the god could destroy even *him*? It didn't make sense. Unless…

I sprang to my feet, startling the three of them. "I think I know what he's doing."

"Horus?" Silas replied and came around the table to where I stood.

"Yeah," I said. "Everything he does is for show, to pull the attention to himself. To make everyone love and worship him. He's narcissistic, yes, but not suicidal. I think…" I mulled it over for another second, "He wanted to make it look like his brother killed the king just to rouse up chaos. And I think he's hoping to release Set so he can defeat him in the eyes of the people. To save them from themselves. An act of bravery like that would definitely garner their love."

They took in my words with heaviness. Isis filled her glass again and stared mindlessly into the distance as she drank from it. Anubis paced thoughtfully while Silas collapsed tiredly into a chair.

"You're right," he breathed. "God, why didn't I see it before?" His fists clenched in his lap. "He truly is a moron, isn't he?"

"It won't work, though," Isis chimed in, her cheeks flush with wine. "Like I said, only an elder god can defeat another elder god. Horus will fail."

"And you're certain you can't do it?" Anubis asked her.

She looked at her nephew, an apologetic expression twisted across her face. "I'm afraid so. You know how it works. We draw strength from our counterparts. Mine has been dead for thousands of years and my power has struggled to replenish after what I did to Set."

No one had a reply. A heavy sense of doom made its

way around the space, pressing down on their shoulders. Isis poured herself yet another drink, and I was grateful she sat on the other side of the large table. I don't think I could handle the luring stench of alcohol, especially in a time like this. And to witness her succumb to the promise it gave made me want to give in, too.

But I couldn't. Not now, not when they all needed me.

I sat at a table circled with the same gods I grew up studying and worshipping, seeing them now in a whole new light. So human, they were. With their worries and broken hearts. Too ready to accept the oncoming fate that Horus was about to rain down on us all.

But it hadn't happened yet. Horus was still in the city. We had time.

"Well," I said, the sound of my voice cutting through the layer of miserable silence that filled the room. They all turned to me. "That just leaves us with one option."

Silas reached up from his chair and wrapped an arm around my waist, pulling me near. "What are you talking about?"

I sucked in a deep breath. This could be the craziest idea, but it's all we had.

"We find Set's grain of sand before Horus does and hide it where he can never find it."

CHAPTER FIFTEEN

I gasped as I stumbled forward from the portal door into the dark hallway of the colony. We had a plan, but time was not on our side if Horus' plan was already in motion. We had to hurry. We determined Isis should stay behind in her palace, to keep the appearance that everything is normal in case Horus came sniffing around. If he found her gone, the paranoid rat might catch on that we knew what he's up to.

Our footsteps echoed off the walls, mixed with our anxious breaths until we reached a fork in the corridors. Anubis spun around.

"Alright," he said. "You guys know what to do, right?"

Silas nodded dutifully. "We'll gather supplies while you fetch some transportation. Then we meet at the mouth of

Osiris' temple."

"Good," he replied and then set his gaze on me. "Are you sure you want to come? This journey could prove to be…difficult."

My spine straightened, and I leaned closer to Silas. "Where he goes, I go. We're all in this together." I sighed nervously. "I just wish we didn't have to trek across the desert to do it."

"It's too risky to take the portal doors," Silas reminded. "Isis destroyed the entrance to the temple where the grain of sand is buried. We don't know the damage done inside or if the portal doors there are intact. We could get stuck in some kind of limbo."

"It's alright," Anubis assured me. "With my expert tracking skills and Isis' directions, I'll get us there in no time." He paused and smoothed a hand over his silky black ears. "We just have to get there before Horus does."

We split up to tackle our assigned tasks, and I hauled Silas along as we cut right through the heart of the colony. The Great Hall. But I never considered the time of day and a meal was in session. The place was jam packed with Star People and the heavy aroma of delicious foods.

We kept our heads down and quickened our pace, but it wasn't enough. Eirik shot up from their seat and zoomed over to us.

"Andie!" they said and stepped in my path. "Where on

earth have you been? You were supposed to stay with your father while I grabbed my medical supplies."

My mind spun as the events of the last couple of days circled around. God, it felt like eons had passed since Eirik and I escaped Horus' palace. So much had happened in the hours since. Like binding my soul to the man I loved for all eternity. My cheeks flushed as I met Silas' knowing sideways glance, and a warmth bubbled up from my gut. We never got the chance to relish in it, and I ached to drag him off to my room where we could celebrate together.

But we had more pressing matters to worry about first.

"I'm sorry," I told my friend. Shadow scurried across the floor then and circled around my ankles like an excited cat. "Something came up. I didn't have time to come find you."

Eirik scrutinized our body language with curiosity. "And now?"

Silas and I exchanged a sigh. "We're about to head out across the desert to–" He cautiously glanced around at all the prying ears and lowered his tone as he leaned in toward Eirik. "My brother is about to do something colossally stupid, and we have to prevent him from succeeding. The fate of the city, of the *world*, depends on it."

Eirik's arms stiffened at their sides. "If Andie's going on a dangerous journey, then I should be with her." Their silver eyes pleaded and then looked to me with concern.

"You may need my help."

"While having you close by definitely makes me feel safer," I replied. "I need you to stay here and protect my Dad. If…if Horus beats us to his goal, then chaos will unleash on the city." *Literally.* "If things go bad, I need you to swear to get him to safety. Can I trust you to do that?"

Eirik raised their silky white chin high. "Of course. I'll protect Alistair with my life."

I don't know what came over me, but I flung myself into Eirik's chest and wrapped my arms around them. Never in my life had another being sworn themselves to me like that. Aside from Dad and Silas, of course. I never really felt what it was like to have friends. The ride or die kind. And now, here in the past with people like Eirik and Anubis, I finally understood it. The dynamic of that true human connection. I needed it.

Shadow's clawed hand wrapped around my leg and a warmth spread upward. He let out a stream of pitchy chirps as I bent down and lovingly smoothed the top of his head.

"You should stay back, too," I told him. Knowing he wanted to come with me. "Help Eirik and my dad. They'll need you if things get too dangerous." I held his little lizardy face in my palm, and he nestled into it for a moment before scuttling off into the crowd.

I stood up and turned to Silas, my chest expanding

with a heavy breath of anticipation.

"Alright." I managed a smile. "Let's go save the world."

***

The three of us trekked across the scorching desert sands on the backs of sturdy donkeys for the better part of the day. The sun was finally beginning its descent and baked my skin from the side rather than from above. Even with the aid of donkeys and the cover of Eirik's special cooling fabric, I was still exhausted. The dry heat baked me from the inside out, and I cursed Silas and Anubis for seeming to be unaffected by it.

I grabbed my water canister and emptied the last into my parched mouth.

"Need a break?" Silas asked as his steed sidled up next to mine. We'd begun the journey with speed, but eventually slowed to a comfortable trot to give the animals a break. "We can stop if you need to."

I shook my head. Too stubborn to admit it. "No, we have to keep going."

"Andie," he said worriedly. "It's a two-day journey. We have to stop at some point, anyway."

I ignored him and motioned to Anubis up ahead. He'd been quiet and distant the whole time. "How's he doing?" I asked. "I mean, it's *his* father we're trying to keep in the ground, after all."

"He'll be alright," Silas replied and stared at his cousin's back. "He's always had us. His family. Those that love him. Anubis has always fit better with me and my parents."

I chewed at my lip as my donkey dutifully trotted along. "Why did Set kill Osiris, anyway?"

His mouth turned down at the corners. "Because my father banished Set's wife and buried her at the bottom of the ocean."

"What? Why would he do *that*?" I thought for a moment, recalling everything I'd studied about these gods. Set's wife and counterpart was Nephthys. The Goddess of Death, Isis' opposite.

"Nephthys was mad," he replied. "Absolutely insane. She tried to kill my mother out of petty jealousy. So, naturally, my father retaliated."

"Christ, your family desperately needs therapy."

Silas chuckled sadly. "Yeah." He fell silent in thought. "The whole thing created this huge rift in our family. Set was enraged. Nephthys was the only being he truly cared about. So, he killed my father. Isis was the force to end it all, but now she's the only one left of the five elder gods."

My head lowered with a frown. "That must be painfully lonely. To have your family all dead and banished like that."

Silas shrugged indifferently and gripped the reins of his

donkey. "She did what she had to do in order to protect her children."

Anubis stopped and turned his donkey around. His pointed ears twitched as he looked up at the sky. "We should make camp for the night. The sun is going down. If we get some rest, we can finish the journey in the early hours of the morning when it's cooler."

Silas gave me a smug grin, and I rolled my eyes before nudging my donkey to follow Anubis over to a small patch of trees in the distance. We tied the three mules under the shade of long fronds near the edge of a small rushing creek and began unpacking supplies to set up a place to rest for the night.

Silas got a little fire going while I secured a tent made of a large thick linen. Anubis stood near the edge of the oasis and stared thoughtfully out toward the horizon. I wondered what he was thinking about, so worried like that. Did he long for his banished parents? Or did he want them in the ground just as much as everyone else did? Anubis was always a little stoic to himself. He rarely expressed much other than discontent for my behavior sometimes. But I considered him a friend, and I felt like that consideration was reciprocated now.

I sat down on the warm grass and breathed in a fresh dose of air, cooling with the setting sun. An orangey glow filtered down over the earth and cast us all in a golden hue. It made the gods I travelled with that much more otherworldly and I sat there admiring their untouchable perfection. Silas' smooth, sand colored skin and his lithe muscles that moved underneath. Anubis' stunning gilded veins that crawled over the pitch-black skin of his body, reflected subtly as flecks in the silky fur that covered his head.

Being around them gave me hope. Hope for the future, *my* future. I was building something here, slowly. And even though Horus was intent on destroying it all before I had the chance to achieve it, part of me remained settled because I would fight to my last breath to protect it. *Them.* Those I cared for here in this time.

Suddenly, something rustled in the bushes at my side and I jumped back with a startle. My heart raced and a new sweat broke out over my skin as I stared into the darkness. The thick foliage ruffled as something moved through it, low to the ground. But my heart calmed when my reptilian pet emerged and collapsed on the grass.

"Shadow!" I cried and crawled over to him. His skin was dry and cracked, his chest heaved with desperate breaths. I pulled him into my lap. "Did you follow us all this way?" I stuck my finger in his little grip and it warmed. "Oh, buddy, I know. I love you, too. But I wanted you to stay back where it was safe."

I carried him over to the creek and washed his dirty

skin, letting the water trickle into his mouth. Soon, he drank on his own and I knew he'd be just fine.

Silas came over and crouched down next to me. "What's baby Yoda doing here?"

I playfully slapped at his arm. "He followed us." My fingers gently scratched the area between the creature's ears. "I told him to stay behind, but I should have known. He has no one. Eirik told me they haven't seen any more of his kind around." My shoulders slumped. "I'm all he's got."

Silas stretched out his long legs toward the edge of the creek. "Determined little bugger, isn't he?" He wrapped an arm around my neck and hauled me in for a kiss. I melted at the soft touch on my mouth, let mine linger there until he grinned. "But I know the feeling."

"What do you mean? Of being alone?" I asked and began untying my boots. "Your entire family is here."

"They're your family now, too. You know?" The words came out almost worriedly. "And it's not just you and your dad. It's *us*. It's my mother." He glanced over at Anubis. "My cousin. My flesh and blood." His hand slid across his chest and rested over his heart. "And now my soul. It's all yours."

My unreliable heart gave away my emotions, and I felt my whole face fill with warmth. Who was I to deserve this? A man, a god, who regarded me so highly. Words evaded me. I kicked off my grungy boots and dipped my feet in the trickling water. The rush of calm that blanketed my whole body was almost too much to bear.

"Are you sure you're ready to put up with me for the rest of eternity?" I said quietly and fixed my stare on Shadow, sniffing around the creek's edge for bugs while my toes lapped in the water.

Silas' hand crawled through the patch of grass between us and our fingers looped together. I met his gaze. Green and gold twirled together like ancient gemstones, and my pulse quickened.

The corner of his mouth twitched. "Andie Godfrey, I'd love you for eternity no matter what. In both life and death." He sucked in a deep breath and released it just as quickly. "Part of me recognized that the moment we met. Something in my soul just *clicked*. But the age difference…"

I chortled. "You're barely three years older than me."

"Silas is, yes," he replied and smiled cheekily. "But Amun has been alive a few more millennia than you."

I cocked my head to the side mockingly. "Funny. One would think you'd be, oh, what's the word I'm looking for?" I stifled the laugh that bubbled up. "Smarter? Wiser?"

Silas shoved me back, and I laid on the grass behind me as he loomed over. Our laughter mixed beautifully, a sound that settled my soul into a frequency of content and something else. Confidence? Eagerness? No. I knew what it was. *Hope*. Silas gave me the hope I needed to live up to my potential. To kick my demons to the curb and move on with my life in the way it should have always been.

But guilt touched the pit of my stomach and I pushed at his chest as I sat up.

"What's the matter?" he asked.

I reached into the inside pocket of my jacket and pulled out my soul stone. The gorgeous ruby sat heavily in my palm. "Part of me feels bad, though. For Dad. He doesn't have this back-up plan that I do." My bottom lip stung as I chewed a little too far. The metallic tinge of open flesh touched my tongue. "I should have made him go back home."

Silas flung an arm around my back and hugged me close. His lips nestled in my hair, kissing the top of my head. "Alistair is stubborn, loyal, and would never have left his only child here in the past."

A weak smile tugged at the corner of my mouth. "Yeah, I guess you're right."

"Of course I am," he replied coyly. "Must be those few million years I have on you."

I chuckled and leaned into him, letting my back mould to the shape of his chest. He wasn't wrong. I knew, deep down, Dad never would have left no matter how much I insisted. Not only was I here, but this was everything he'd ever wanted. To experience his passion, his purpose in life through firsthand experiences.

Still…it didn't lessen my worry.

Did I do the right thing? Should I have forced it? Dare say…even sent him back against his will? At least he'd be safe. Alive. But now it was too late. Dad was stuck here in this wild and dangerous past with me. My selfishness told me not to push, but will that same greed be what leads my father to his death?

CHAPTER SIXTEEN

The dying fire allowed a stark coolness to touch my skin and coax me from sleep. I didn't open my eyes, though. I was too exhausted. It turned out the Gatekeeper to the Underworld snores like a hog on its back, so I slipped out of our shared tent and curled up by the flames during the wee hours of the night.

I shifted on the half of the blanket that was beneath me and flung my arm over my half-opened eyes to prevent the coming sun from seeping in through the cracks. The heavy sheet of night still touched everything, holding the world in a navy dream. But the pinch of orange on the horizon oozed over the sands. Thankfully, the cover of trees overhead left our little oasis in the shadows and I longed for a few more minutes of sleep.

But something pinched my lower back, and I grumbled as I rolled over again. It was probably a root or a rock. My eyelids were weighty again and the gentle fog of sleep pulled me in just as another pinch jolted me awake, this time on my lower leg. I sat up, groggy and immediately grumpy, searching the blanket around my leg for the culprit.

But there was nothing.

I couldn't go back to sleep now. My grimy hands wiped over the tight skin of my face, tender from the sun's exposure of the previous day. I grabbed one of my boots I'd left off to the side and—out of habit from my lifetime growing up with an archaeologist father—dumped it upside down to expel any critters who'd slept there during the night. I expected nothing to fall out, but something did. A tiny flash of gold, so quick I hardly caught it. The thing hit the ground and disappeared in the blink of an eye.

Then something pinched my shoulder. My hip. My thigh. I swatted at my body as panic chased away any remnants of sleep. But I couldn't see what was biting me. Another painful nip on my back and I hopped to my feet with a yelp.

Shadow scurried across the ground, emerging from the tent, and chased something into a bush. He waddled back out with something clamped in his jaw. It wriggled, catching the glow of hot embers from the firepit, and gleamed like a piece of gold jewelry.

I stepped closer, eliciting a low growl from Shadow over the possession of his kill. I narrowed my eyes, examining the two ends dangling from his toothy snarl. A curled tail and two lobster claws. A cold fright struck my veins, and I stumbled back with a gasp.

"Scorpions," I whispered in disbelief. The ground suddenly came to life with a golden wave of the lethal pests as they pushed out from the bushes. My eyes widened. "Oh my God!"

I grabbed my other boot and hauled them on with haste before I began stamping madly at the swarm. The thick linen of the tent ruffled, and my two travel companions burst from it in a spiral of their own cries. Silas swatted at his legs and he hopped about, while Anubis laid down a hefty stomp and caught one pest underfoot. He plucked it between his finger and thumb, brought it to his face to examine.

"Your bother," he said to Silas and tossed the golden scorpion to the side. "He must be sending plagues to stop us from getting to the temple before him."

"Grab our things and get out!" Silas ordered and stuffed my bag in my arms. "Go, get a respectful distance away."

I shook my head in confusion. "Why? What are you–"

"Just move it, Andie!" he bellowed.

I scrambled to grab as much as I could and called for

Shadow to follow as Anubis and I untied our donkeys and led them out onto the sand outside the oasis. I stood, anxious breath burning in my lungs as I watched Silas blow on the dying embers. A flame caught, and he moved his hands in the air, as if…*pulling* the fire toward him. It grew, and he manipulated the flame into a roaring fire that hovered in the air with no anchor. Silas swung his arms and tossed the flames around, setting ablaze to the entire oasis. Shadow scrambled from my grip and ran over to join him, blowing streams of glorious reds and oranges at the ground, reducing everything to a billowing inferno.

Silas stumbled backward, catching himself, and joined us where we stood watching in utter awe. Or, well, I was anyway. Anubis' staid expression didn't falter an inch toward wonder. As if seeing his cousin create a flame thrower out of thin air was nothing out of the ordinary.

And perhaps it wasn't. Clearly, I still had a lot to learn about Silas' powers.

"So, Horus knows our plan, I assume?" I said.

Silas' lungs heaved, and he turned to us. Anger splashed across his face. "Horus has eyes everywhere. But at least we know he's still behind us."

Anubis gazed out to the horizon and the coming sun. "We have time if we start now. We can make it by mid-afternoon."

I took a step and immediately winced from the searing

pain that stung like a bolt of electricity. I bent over and grappled with the hem of my pants leg and hauled it up. A festering purple lump protruded just above my ankle.

"How many times were you stung?" Anubis asked.

I shrugged through the raking sensation that suddenly coursed through my blood. "A few."

With a disgruntled mutter, he turned to his mule and opened one of the saddlebags. Silas bent to examine the wound closer while his cousin brought over a jar of what looked like moldy slime.

"This is a topical salve for poisons," Anubis told me, and twisted the lid on the jar. "Eirik gave me some supplies before we left. This should extract most of the venom. At least enough to get us back to the colony." He exchanged a knowing look with Silas. "If left untreated, these stings would have surely killed her."

My heart thudded against its cage.

Silas sprung to his feet while Anubis coated my scorpion stings with the raunchy ointment, and I immediately felt the relief of the poison being pulled from the wounds.

"I'm going to kill my brother and bury his amulet at the bottom of the deepest ocean." He clenched a fist as the words seethed from his mouth.

I patted his arm and smiled through the pain. "One crisis at a time. Let's go find a magical grain of sand and prevent the God of Chaos and Destruction from destroying the world first."

***

The second half of our journey went by much faster than the first. The push of urgency was fresh and alive, moving us along as we followed Anubis' expert tracking ability. He rode his mule as if he knew exactly where to go and, the more I thought about it, he probably did. These gods possessed powers unlike anything I could have ever dreamed of. Like the stuff of movies or fantasy novels.

Shadow sat content in my arms as I held the reins of my donkey with one hand. I tried to ignore the stark silence that hummed around Silas just a couple feet to my right. He was pissed, I got that. But I worried for him. This eternal rivalry between him and his brother was unhealthy, to say the least. One of them was bound to end up dead, and I constantly battled with the possibility that it might be the man I loved.

Anubis hauled back on the leather reins and his donkey came to a halt. His jackal head sniffed at the air and he closed his eyes for a moment before turning to look back at us.

"It's here," he said with stone cold certainty.

I glanced around but there was nothing only sand as far as the eye could see. A warm breeze tickled my face and the hot afternoon sun kissed my skin where the salve didn't cover. I tugged at the edges of the cooling fabric of Eirik's old cloak and shielded my face, not wanting it to burn any more than it already had.

"Are you sure?" Silas asked him.

Anubis nodded and hopped down from his mount. He circled a spot in the sand. "How deep did your mother say she buried the temple?"

Silas joined him on the ground. "Deep."

"Can you do it?" his cousin replied.

He bent his knees and squat over the ground as his fingers stuck in the sand, pushing and sinking up to his wrists. His eyes closed, and a calmness washed over his face for a moment before they flew open again.

"Yes," Silas assured us. "I can feel it. Deep beneath the surface." He examined the area widely. "Stand back. Way back."

Anubis and I led the donkeys back a way, while keeping Silas in our sights. Shadow played and dug in the sand near my feet, totally oblivious to what we were doing. But then I realized, I didn't really know what was about to happen myself. Silas remained perched in the sand; his fingers stuck deep beneath the surface. The air tightened and vibrate with a strange energy. All emanating outward from my boyfriend. I watched intently, but the sound of a falcon crying in the distance stole my attention and I whipped my head around in search of the bird I've now come to fear.

"What's the matter?" Anubis asked.

"Did you hear that?"

He lowered his head and peered around. "Hear what?"

I strained to listen again, my eyes scanning the blank skies. But there was nothing. I shook my head. "Nothing. Must have been my mind. Maybe the heat is getting to me."

"Well, won't be much longer now," he replied. "Amun will unearth the entrance in no time."

"Is *that* what he's doing?"

But Anubis didn't get the chance to reply. Just like the dense air around us, the sand beneath our feet hummed, the mild vibrations tickling up through my legs. Shadow stopped rooting around in the dirt and his ears flattened against his head as he scurried over to me. The pulsations increased, getting deeper and louder with every passing second.

Suddenly, a small hole formed just a few yards from where Silas hunched, and sand trickled inside it. Soon, a wide mouth opened in the ground and more sand poured down inside it, like a slow releasing drain. The hole grew bigger and bigger, with a terrifying amount of sand billowing into it and I realized the rim was opening toward him.

"Silas!" I cried and bolted after him without a second thought.

"Andie! Stop!" Anubis called.

But it was too late. The ground beneath me gave way like play doh and my body hit the cascading sand like a sack of potatoes. It sucked me inside, unrelenting and impossible to escape. I scrambled and clawed in a futile attempt to climb back up, but it was no use.

The hole must have been fifty feet wide now, and I hurled toward a dark pit. More sand pushed from above and I glanced up in a panic to find two more bodies sliding in the same direction I was headed.

I was nearing the bottom, a black void too far down for sunlight to reach, and I covered my head protectively with my arms as I shot inside a narrow rectangular opening and tumbled to the bottom of a stone cased entryway. I landed on my back, knocking the wind right out of my lungs, and gasped for air as I struggled to my feet. Sand continued to trickle down and around the entry, most of it missing the open doorway that sat at an odd upward angle.

Soon, Anubis and Silas tumbled inside, Shadow not far behind. He scrambled to his little feet as he coughed up bits of sand and shook away what coated his skin. Anubis brushed at his clothes and narrowed his eyes at me in the near darkness.

"It's a wonder you've made it this far in life, you know that?"

My cheeks flushed. "Sorry about that. I thought Silas

was going to get sucked down in the hole."

"And yet," Anubis gestured widely at his cousin, "here he is. Alive."

I rolled my eyes. The guy could be so uptight sometimes.

Silas was on his feet and by my side. He shook the sand from his hair and dusted it off his clothes. "It's fine. We're all fine. Now, let's get what we came for before my brother finds us here."

He grabbed a thick piece of wood sticking out of the wall and tore part of his shirt to wrap around the end. Then pointed the tip down toward Shadow.

"Care to light the way?" Silas asked the creature.

Shadow cooed and chirped, then sucked in a deep breath of air before blowing out a small stream of fire. The end of the torch caught and the cave-like temple around us suddenly became alight with a dim golden glow. The firelight refracted off the jagged stone walls, and we crept deeper and deeper inside. Aside from endless hieroglyphs, the place was nearly empty. No statues, no sarcophaguses, no furniture. Nothing. As if it had been cleaned out before Isis sunk it to the bottom of the desert.

I trailed along, not really sure exactly what we were looking for. My gaze raked over the beautiful and neglected images carved into the walls.

"Did Isis say where it was? Or what it looks like?" I

asked, my voice nothing but a deep echo through the chambers.

"Yeah," Silas replied, just a couple of feet in front of me. "She said to look for a Malek Box."

"What's that?" I couldn't take my eyes off the hieroglyphs. There was something familiar about the symbols and some of the words.

Anubis glanced over his shoulder. "A small metallic box that can fit in your hand."

We turned a corner, and I stopped to narrow my gaze at another image. "Hey, wait." I waved Silas back. "Bring that torch here."

He held it up to the wall and the three of us gasped in unison.

Anubis tilted his head as he examined. "Is that…"

"A Tanin warrior." The words came out in a whisper across Silas' lips as he stared at the giant reptilian humanoid, clad in armor.

"I thought Tanins didn't really take root here," I said, remembering what Eirik had told me.

"They didn't," Anubis replied. "That we know of. But look at this." He pointed to another wall, one covered in what looked like a map swathed in strange, yet familiar, symbols.

Shadow crawled up in my arms and reached out toward the wall. His little palm pressed against it and he let out a saddened coo. A reptilian monarch wore a gaudy head piece while leading a ship across the sea where it seemed another temple like this one awaited. The shapes of the bodies of land resembled that of the continents I knew on this world. But, as I traced the story of pictures with my eyes, I realized the creatures exited their ship on the other side of the world, but with the faces of men.

Human men.

"My god," I choked out. "Is this saying…they were… *shapeshifters?*"

"So, they came here, after all," Silas spoke with uncertain awe.

I looked at Shadow in my arms. "But where did they all go?"

Anubis clapped Silas' upper arm. "That may be a question for your mother. But right now, we have more pressing matters."

"Yes, you're right," he agreed and began pacing the large room we were in. The single torch was dimming as he walked the perimeter, glancing inside the only doorway other than the one we entered through. "This is it. There's nothing more except two portal doors in this large closet."

I let Shadow hop down to the floor as I craned my neck and searched around for a sign of…anything. "Well, it has to be here, then. Keep looking."

Shadow's padded feet tapped against the cold stone and

he moved within the space as if he'd been here before, with purpose. He climbed up on a stone ledge and puffed a flame that immediately caught fire to a trough of some sort of oil, causing a ribbon of fire to circle around the room.

I smiled at the creature. "You're just full of surprises, aren't you?"

He chirped happily.

I examined the chamber with fresh eyes, in the generous firelight, and noticed a small square amongst the many carvings on the wall. The line around it thicker and deeper than the rest. Like a tile without grout. I walked over and touched my hand to it and noted how it felt loose to the touch. Like I could just pull it out.

"Guys," I said. "Could this be what we're looking for?"

They came over and stood on either side of me while I gently pushed on the square, realizing then that it wasn't made of stone like the wall, but of a weird, soft black metal. It popped out enough that I could secure my fingers around it.

I looked at Silas. "Do I just pull it out? What if–" I chewed at my lip, wondering if I was being ridiculous. "Would it be…booby trapped?"

He chuckled lightly and shook his head at his confused cousin. "No, I doubt it," he told me. "My mother would have warned us, I'm sure."

With a deep breath, I pinched the box with all my fingers

and pulled it from its perfect hole in the wall. It slid without resistance and I held the surprisingly light box in my hand.

"Should we open it to make sure?" I asked.

Anubis stared at it, a distant look in his eyes. I held the key to his father's resurrection in my palm. I wondered then, what he truly thought of it all. What side he fell on when it came to his family's dysfunctional matters.

"Are you alright?" I asked him.

He shivered away the daze and took a step back. "Yes. It's just…" His arms crossed tightly. "It's difficult to have a parent whom you both love and fear."

Silas and I stood in silence, letting him have a moment with his own resolve.

"But that's neither here nor there," Anubis added with a hint of positivity in his tone. He straightened his back proudly. "This is a Malek Box, it's surely the one we came for. Opening it could release my father in his elemental form. If that grain of sand comes in contact with another, that's all he'd need. We can't risk it." His nostrils at the tip of his black nose flared with a deep breath. "Let's get it to secure location."

"No need, cousin," a voice sounded from behind.

I spun around, my heart already flown into a panic, and my throat squeezed with the rush of fear that suddenly coursed through my body. Horus stood there, smug and waiting. Silas stepped in front of me protectively, and I peered around his shoulder as the god stepped closer.

A wild, sneering grin spread across his face. "I'll take it off your hands."

CHAPTER SEVENTEEN

It's crazy how fast things can change right in front of your eyes. And when it's for the worst, it's even faster. The world around me closed in, my ears filled with the quickened pulse of my life force, and I swayed on my feet. Pushing back against the heavy blanket of nausea that threatened to push me down.

Silas widened his stance and braced himself between his brother and me. His wide shoulders heaved under the thin cover of his linen shirt. From this close, I could feel the air that touched his body humming, the way it did when he was about to use his powers.

Horus swung a leg in front of the other as he confidently paced the area between us and the exit. He clucked his tongue and waggled a finger at his brother. "Now, now. I wouldn't do that if I were you. Wouldn't want to accidentally let dear old uncle out now, would we?"

Silas guffawed. "Isn't that what you want?"

He shrugged carelessly. "Yes, but I'm not sure I'd like to do it down here." He motioned at the cavernous space around us. "Who knows how sound this ancient structure is? And, I don't know about you, but I don't fancy being crushed to death by a cave-in." His wide hands smoothed over the ornate chest piece he wore over a cream tunic. "I've grown fond of this body over the last few thousand years."

"What are you really doing?" Anubis seethed.

Horus feigned surprise. "I thought that was rather obvious. I needed to find Set but hadn't the first idea where to look. I knew my mother would never tell me; I've tried everything to get inside her head. She's stubborn." His dark eyes narrowed on me. "It's frustrating." I swallowed nervously as he continued. "But I knew she'd tell you. Especially if the location had been compromised."

Silas' fists clenched at his sides. "You wanted me to hear you discussing your plan, didn't you? It was all a trick."

His brother stared unapologetically. "Are you surprised?"

In unison, the three of us replied in defeat, "No."

"You can't resurrect my father," Anubis said and stepped forward. "He's nothing but chaos and destruction, and he's had thousands of years being angry at the world. He'll destroy *everything*."

"That's the plan," Horus replied as he examined the hieroglyphs on the surrounding walls with a sense of boredom. He cringed at the cacophony of protests we threw at him. "Easy, easy. I'll put him back. I just need to…borrow him for a bit."

I'd had enough. My impatience stomped down my fear. "But that's the thing, Horus. You won't be able to put him back." I peered over Silas' protective shoulder. "You're not strong enough."

He flashed me a glare that could cut through glass. "Do *not* tell me what I can and cannot do. I will release Set on the world, and they *will* beg for me to save them from themselves. And when they watch me destroy the God of Chaos and Destruction, they'll worship at my feet and hand over their hearts without question."

"But that's not love!" I cried, frustrated at his stubbornness. I took a step forward, but Silas' arm held me back. "That's *fear*."

For a split second, I could see a hint of sadness flash in his eyes, but his expression hardened. "I see no difference." Horus fixed on the cube in Silas' hand. "Now, hand over the Malek Box."

"Never," Silas replied and stuffed it in the satchel that hung across his chest.

"Then you leave me no choice, brother," Horus replied and readied himself for an attack.

"Very well, then." Silas stomped his foot and his golden staff shot up from the floor where he caught it in his hand without breaking his stare down with Horus.

The temple immediately filled with noise as the two dove into a brawl. Thick waves of energy blasted back and forth, knocking one another into a wall or scraping across the stone floor. I wanted to help, to jump in and break up the fight, but what could I do, really? A mere human girl with zero fighting skills had no chance of even coming between two clashing gods.

Anubis stood on one side of the room, hunched and waiting for the chance to jump in, while I hovered in a corner on the other side with Shadow at my feet. If only I'd put the cube in my backpack, I could make a run for it while they distracted Horus. But that wasn't the case, and I stood helplessly in wait.

In the blink of an eye, Horus grabbed hold of Silas' arms and let out a guttural roar as he spun him around, putting himself between me and Silas. My heart pounded in my chest and I didn't have the chance to even scream as Horus moved with a blinding speed and I was in his grasp. My back to his chest, a knife to my throat.

"Andie!" Silas cried, but came to a screeching halt when the blade tightened against my skin and I let out a wince.

I could feel it break the surface and a warm trickle made its way down my neck, causing the gold flecks in Silas' panicked eyes to gleam intensely. Shadow growled from below and I heard the distinct *thwomp* of something kicking him out of the way. His little body crumbled to the floor a few feet away, and I whined in place, unable to move. Tears streamed down over my cheeks, but a dose of panic shot through me when I noticed Silas and Anubis moved toward us.

"No!" I pleaded with a gurgle. "Don't. Just stay back."

The hand that wasn't holding the knife to my throat stuck out, palm up. "The cube," Horus demanded neatly. "*Now.*"

He hesitated, but only waited a moment before he reached for his bag.

"No, Silas, don't!" My eyes widened, begging him not to do it. "Just leave. Get out of here." Cautiously, I gently patted the pocket that we both knew held my soul stone.

Silas wavered, glancing back and forth between his cousin and me. From the corner of my eye, I could see that Anubis held a squirming Shadow in his arms. My heart relaxed knowing he was okay.

The room held in suspended wait, none of us truly knowing what the right move was. Horus chuckled and tightened his arm around me. But not the blade.

"I guess she doesn't mean as much to you as I thought,"

he taunted his brother.

That was it. I was tired of being held at knife point or constantly being thrust to the median of danger. I was done feeling helpless. I bent my knee and brought the heel of my boot crushing down on Horus' sandaled feet. His body tensed as he seethed in pain, and I ran for the exit. Silas tossed me his bag, and I gripped it tightly as I ran for an escape.

But it wasn't enough.

A blast of cold energy bounced off the walls, reverberating back and knocking me to the floor. My ears rang, and I struggled to look behind me, only to witness Horus let out another blow of power, and watched the others smash into the stone walls, causing cracks to form all the way to the ceiling as they crumbled to the floor.

I pushed to my feet, determined to keep running, but Horus leaped across the room and snatched the bag from my arms. I tried to grab at it, but he swatted me away and hastily ripped into it to retrieve the cube. His fingers worked quickly to twist the different sides, and I realized it was designed like a Rubik's cube.

"Brother!" Silas cried and pushed to his feet. "You don't know what you're doing!"

I don't know what brought it on, but my ears warmed as the room dimmed around me. It was just me and Horus, standing together in a void space suspended in motion. A strange sense of calmness washed over me, and I gently laid a hand on Horus' arm, our eyes locking.

"You'll kill us all," I whispered firmly.

As if entranced by the sudden tender touch, he waited a beat, the cube still unopened but now pulsing with energy like a heartbeat. Our eyes unblinking as they remained fixed together. A drop of hope entered my veins and I clung to it with a clawing desperation, banking on Horus doing the right thing. Willing him to do so.

But the cube itself made one last click that cut through the silence of anticipation and we both looked at it with wide eyes while a single grain of sand fell from it. A sliver of regret flashed in his bulbous brown eyes and he dropped the cube. The sound a clamor of metal on stone. Four heaving sets of lungs filled the echoed space with uncertainty as we waited, unknowing and helpless as to what to expect.

At first, nothing happened, but then the air changed. Sucking in on itself and syphoning the oxygen from the room. Sand billowed in from the only door that led to the exit, blowing and twirling, scratching my baked skin. I held up an arm to shield my face and Silas ran to my side as Horus stood as still as a statue, enwrapped in his own doing.

Silas enveloped me in his arms, protecting me from the storm of sand that now whipped around the cavern. Anubis, with Shadow in his grasp, huddled in. We waited, for that was all we could do. Horus stood between us and the exit and I knew we could easily blow past him, but the amount of sand increased, and I couldn't even open my eyes. All I could do was brace myself against Silas' warm chest.

The air tightened until my lungs burned for breath, but I didn't dare open my mouth. Sand filled my nostrils and blinded my senses until I nearly reached a breaking point. But in that moment, that split second between holding on by a thread and giving up, everything stopped, and the bits of sand fell from the air.

I gasped for a fresh breath, filled my lungs and opened my eyes to look up at Silas whose expression paled as he stared over my head. I spun in his hold and froze. There, in the middle of the massive space, stood a figure, taller than anyone else in the room. The shape of a man formed in sand, a girth of shoulders heaved in anger, and he slowly turned to face us as his skin smoothed to a soft brown.

Set.

He stood between us and Horus, rage vibrating around him. His intense stare examined the room, changing and narrowing as his gaze fell on Horus. I could see the pieces of his new reality clicking into place. The god turned and grimaced at the sight of his son, not even granting him the dignity of a greeting after so many thousands of years, then sizing up Silas with curiosity. This was a body he'd never seen before. His stare dropped to the amulet around Silas' neck, and realization flashed across his face as his mouth turned up in a scowl.

"*Where*," his deep voice boomed off the walls, "Is. Isis?"

CHAPTER EIGHTEEN

"Father!" Anubis pleaded, but didn't dare step away from his place near the back of the room with us.

My heart sank as I witnessed the fear in his helpless expression, in the way he barely moved. A fear no son should have towards his father. Any doubt I had in my mind about where he stood on the status of Set fled my mind.

"You can't do this," he continued. "You must calm down."

"Calm down?" Set's words ground against my ears. Then he chuckled, low and menacing. "My treacherous son. I assume it wasn't you who freed me?"

Anubis' ear flattened against his head. "No, I'm afraid not."

"It was I who freed you, Uncle," Horus piped in, stealing Set's attention.

Silas held me close and whispered in my ear. "You need to get out of here. Sneak back into that hallway. Take the portal doors back to the colony."

My lips pinched together. "No, I'm not leaving you."

A lock of hair fell down over the sweat beads on his pinched forehead. "Then you're a fool. To stay here would be suicide, Andie. I can't let you do that."

"Then what was the point of making me a soul stone?" I said in a lowered, cautious tone.

Anubis eyed his father deep in conversation with Horus on the other side of the room while he inched back toward us. He leaned in and whispered, "We need to get out of here *now*."

I thumbed at Silas. "Mr. Heroic here won't come."

Silas sighed and looked at his cousin with intent. "Take her."

Without missing a beat, Anubis grabbed me. I tried to protest, but his large hand cupped my mouth, stifling any sort of sound that could catch the attention of Set. Dragging me along, we turned the corner to the closeted hallway behind us and slinked into darkness where it let me go.

"Shhh," he said quickly, stopping me from any sort of retort. He crouched down and peeked around the corner where the others remained. "I wouldn't leave him either, Andie. Trust that. I'll grab him the first chance I can, and we'll jump into those portal doors."

Every ounce of air I inhaled was painful as I struggled to calm the fear that coursed through me. My body wanted to hyperventilate, but I drummed up whatever ounce of bravery I had in me to wait. Shadow gripped the sleeve of my jacket and I gave him a reassuring pat on the head. I scrunched up next to Anubis and joined him in watching his family standing off in a triad of angst.

"Uncle," Horus iterated, "I've brought you back to your elemental form. If you'll allow, I'd like to aid you in the search for your physical body. My mother has hidden–"

"Silence!" The sound of Set's voice was like stone against stone. His arm shot out and he summoned a surge of power that flung Horus into the wall. "I've been trapped for thousands of years. Now I shall take what is mine. Revenge. I'll bring down a reign of chaos and destruction on this planet so mighty that they'll bow at my feet before I kill them all."

"Set, please, if you'd just–" Another wave of energy pushed toward Silas, but he jumped out of the way, bracing himself just a few feet from where we squat in the dark.

Horus scrambled to his feet. "Uncle, I think if you just listen to what I have to say–"

"Enough! There is nothing you can say that I want to

hear. It's time I got my revenge, first with the gods that disgracefully share my blood." Set sneered as new sand appeared and twirled around his form, helping him to grow even larger. His figure loomed over the room, inches from the vaulted ceiling, and he stalked toward Horus with an evil chuckle. "Starting with you, dear nephew."

I watched as pure shock possessed my body, just as Silas and Anubis did, while Set summoned a whirlwind of air and sand, catching Horus in a tornado that lifted him from the floor. He choked and gasped for air, clawing at his throat while his legs flailed beneath him. I couldn't watch, my eyes averted to Silas, but that was just as painful to witness. He stood helplessly as he watched the life being squeezed from his brother. Torment twisted in his glossy expression and I ached to reach out to him. To drag him into the shadows with us where I could keep him safe. But I knew now…

He'd never leave his brother.

My calves burned as I remained crouched next to Anubis, but I didn't dare move. Fear and disbelief of the tragic events playing out before my very eyes held me firmly in place. Horus' elaborate plan turned on him in an instant, and now he was suffering through the last moments of his life. As much as I hated him, it was hard to watch. Tears stung the rims of my eyes and silently spilled over. Set clenched his power, constricting Horus in one last crushing hold, and he leaned in as the billowing sand quietened. I saw his lips moving near Horus' face and I strained to hear the last words he muttered.

"Our secret dies with you."

Horus' body went limp and Set tossed him aside like a piece of trash as he turned to a grieving Silas. Would he do the same to the man I loved? Would I be forced to watch him suffer the same fate as his brother?

"Why?" Silas cried. "You don't have to do this!"

Set sniveled. "Oh, but I want to."

A deep, raspy chuckle rumbled from the god's sandy throat and he bent down to rip Horus' now glowing soul stone from around his neck. He let it sit in his hand, as if testing the weight of it, then crushed his fingers around it.

"No!" The sound squeezed from Silas' mouth with an innocent rawness.

But it was no use. The stone cracked in the god's grip and two pieces fell to the floor. Dull and lifeless. Silas dropped to his knees and buried his face in his hands. I covered my mouth with a trembling hand as I watched. Set took a couple of steps toward him, but then stopped. As if another thought fled through his mind. Then, in another heinous whirlwind of sand and air, Set reduced himself to his pure elemental form and fled the room in a massive wave of living sand.

Immediately, the integrity of the ancient chamber

faltered and everything around us shook. Bits of stone crumbled away from the cracks in the walls, crashing to the floor. Anubis bolted to his feet and ran to Silas.

"Come on!" he yelled. "We have to get out!"

But Silas pushed him away and fumbled over to where his brother's lifeless body lay in a heap on the floor. Anubis hurried after him, and Silas scooped Horus into his arms before turning and rushing back toward the shadowed hallway where I waited anxiously.

The exit on the other side of the cavernous room had already closed off, buried in chunks of stone. The trough of fire broke open and oil spilled onto the floor, igniting everything in a fiery inferno. The cave in was quickly making its way in our direction and I ushered them to move faster.

"Come on! Come on!" I yelled through the chaos and waved my arm frantically.

Anubis and Silas met me in the darkness, and together we all filed into one of the jagged rectangular cut-outs in the wall. Shadow hopped up into my arms and we squeezed together, my eyes pressed shut while more and more stone crumbled around us. The inside of the portal let out a shrieking, cracking noise, and I yelped as I forced my mind to think of where to go.

The colony. Safety. Home.

Just as the last of the temple fell, everything went stark

quiet until we were spit out on the other end and we tumbled forward into a hallway in the colony. The three of us collapsed on the floor, heaving for air, and letting the rapid events that just unfolded organize in our minds.

Shadow scampered over to Silas, whose back curved in a hunch over his brother's dead body. On wobbly arms, I pushed myself up and crawled over to him. Anubis lay on his back, staring at the ceiling in shock. I let him have his peace.

My hand slid over Silas' tense back. "Hey, it's okay. We're all okay."

"How can you say that?" His watery eyes glistened in the dim torchlight.

"Silas, this isn't your fault."

"But it is," he replied weakly. "It's always my fault when it comes to my brother, and now he's gone." A sob bubbled from his throat. "Completely gone."

Anubis sat up with a deep sigh. "Maybe not completely."

Our heads whipped in his direction. "What do you mean?"

"We should find your mother soon, before my father gets a chance. Bring her here to safety," he suggested curtly. Then held out his fist. "But also, so she can fix this." His fingers bloomed and, in his palm, sat the two broken pieces of a rock.

Horus' soul stone.

CHAPTER NINETEEN

Paranoia consumed me as I wore wear lines in the floor of my quarters. Shadow perched on my bed and gnawed at some bread he stole from the Great Hall. Strangely, having him nearby gave me a sense of calmness. A sliver, really. But it was all I had. I kept forcing myself to look at him when the swirling thoughts became too much.

It'd been over an hour since Silas and Anubis left to retrieve Isis and I long passed the level of simply worried. I was full blown freaking out. One half of me plunged into the disaster at hand. How far had Set's rage spread? What were the casualties already? But the other half of me, the one rooted in my own personal fear, worried about bringing Horus back to life. Would he come to his senses and be on our side? Or would we have two homicidal maniacs on our hands?

No, some spark in the back of my mind knew that, no matter how horrible Horus was, he'd never want the people of Egypt to *die*. He desired their affection far too much. The two overwhelming routes of possibilities tugged me every which way and I struggled to hold it together.

I stormed over to the bed and Shadow crawled into my lap as I rocked back and forth. I held him tight to my chest, almost too tight. He squirmed, but never complained, and he released a slow warmth that soothed my chest.

"Does Horus even *deserve* to be saved?" I asked my reptilian friend. "After everything he's done. How he…" My lip trembled at the thought. "How he tortured me for hours. Put a knife to my throat. Held me prisoner for nearly two days."

I swallowed nervously and then yelped as a knock rapped at the door. I dropped Shadow on the blanket and leaped for the handle, hauling it open to find Silas. Disheveled and breathy. He leaned against the door frame and regarded me without a word.

"A-are you okay?" I asked. "What happened? Is your mom safe?"

He tipped his head and motioned down the hall. "She's fine. I'll explain everything later." Silas stood straight with a deep, exhausted sigh. "They're all waiting in my father's temple."

"Wait," I replied, and he looked at me with surprise. "Can we talk first?"

Silas waited a beat, then nodded. "Of course."

He followed me inside and I shut the door before spinning around to face him. "I'm worried about bringing your brother back. I understand that you, for god knows why, *love* him. I do, I truly do." I rubbed my palms against the patchy surface of my jeans. "But he also tortured me. I'm…I'm scared of him, Silas. What if he continues to manipulate you through me? What would that even mean? What would he do to me to get what he wants?"

His hands clung to his hips as he stared at the floor between us. I let him stew the words in his head. Finally, he raked his fingers through his wavy hair. "You're right."

"What?" I wasn't expecting him to cave so soon.

"I know the logic and truth in what you're saying," Silas explained. "But he's still my brother. My counterpart. My blood. We share something that no other Star People share. I'm *made* from him, Andie. Without Horus I'm weaker, and definitely won't stand a chance of defeating Set."

I guffawed and half turned away, arms crossed. "You don't stand a chance regardless, remember? Isis said, only an Elder God can defeat another Elder God."

"Well, maybe two younger ones can," he snapped impatiently.

My brows pinched together. "Are you serious? Anubis? He'd fight against his own father?"

My respect for the guy was building fast. The past two days, he'd shown where his true loyalty lay. Time and time again.

"Of course," he said dismissively and arched a brow at me. "Was that ever in question?"

I shook my head. Exhaustion crept in. My body begged for sleep. "Look, I get it. I know what it's like to feel as if a part of you is missing." He didn't reply, and I heaved a reluctant sigh. "Okay, let's do it."

"Are you sure?" His face was a mask of confusion.

I slid my hands over his crossed arms and smiled warmly up at his weary face. "If it makes you happy."

His fingers brushed my cheek, tucking my hair behind my ear as he leaned in to touch his lips to mine. A simple, but tender move and my heart settled in knowing I could give him this. I could find a way to be okay with Horus' existence, if it meant so much to him.

I just prayed I wouldn't come to regret it.

We headed for Osiris' temple, where Anubis and Isis stood by the stone platform that held up Horus' slack body. It was so weird, seeing him like that. A shell. A lifeless form. He seemed so harmless in this state.

"Andie," Isis spoke my name with a certain motherly sadness. But she greeted me with a smile. "It's good to see you again." She softly turned her head and her fingers grazed her dead son's face. "I just wish it were under better circumstances."

I noticed then, her dishevelled appearance. Still, the ever-ethereal beauty she always was, but with wiry tendrils of wind-blown hair out of place, taught skin around her tired eyes. She also nursed her arm as if it were causing her pain.

What the hell happened out there?

"Are you sure you want to do this?" she asked Silas. "After everything he's done to you in the past?"

He seemed taken aback. "Mother, he's your son."

Her indifferent expression hummed and hawed, and she shrugged sadly. "Yes. And I'll grieve for his death. But I know in my heart that he made the choices that led to his own death." Her trembling fingers smoothed over Horus' stiff chest. "He brought this on himself."

He glanced at Anubis for back-up, and when he got nothing in return, Silas looked to me, searching my face for reassurance. "No matter how angry with one another we may have ever been, we'd never destroy each other's amulets."

I guffawed. "Yeah, just trap you inside it and bury it deep in the desert for thousands of years."

"He could have destroyed it," Silas argued weakly. "But he didn't. He wouldn't." His mossy eyes gleamed with tears. "I can't expect any of you to understand it, but I love him. I do. He's my *brother*."

"And what about Andie?" Anubis piped up, and even I looked at him with surprise. "What does *she* mean to you? Your brother tried to kill her, more than once, might I remind."

Silas grit his teeth together, his fingers mulling together in his tight hands. "And for that he'll pay dearly. I swear." His pitiful gaze fell on me and my heart clenched. I didn't want to come between him and something, someone he cared for. Not like this. His voice softened. "We don't need to resurrect him in his body. If Isis can fix the amulet, then that's where he'll stay."

Hope bloomed in my chest. "Promise?"

He stepped toward me and cupped the side of my neck in his hand before placing a kiss to my forehead. "Promise."

Isis cleared her throat and glanced toward the exit that led out to the other side of the mountain we stood in. "We have little time. Set is wreaking havoc already, in search of Star People." She swallowed nervously. "In search of... me. He'll destroy all of Egypt in a matter of days. Even if I fix the stone, Horus' soul is gone. It'll need to be retrieved and that'll take *time*."

Anubis crossed his muscled arms over his chest. "I have a plan for that. We just need to know if you can fix the stone or not."

She pursed her lips and moved her other hand from inside the long teal robes that hung from her body and opened her palm to reveal the two broken pieces. She stared at them longingly. "I can. But the stone is no good without a soul to put in it. Are you sure you can do it?"

Anubis and Silas exchanged a hesitant but thoughtful glance. "Yes. We have time. His soul has yet to pass beyond. I can retrieve it from the Underworld, from the River of Souls."

A stark memory pinged in my brain, and I suddenly recalled my brief moment in the River of Souls. How I'd been dead. Gone to this world, and the one I knew. Floating along in the glowing current.

"Very well," Isis replied with a single nod. "Let's not waste any more time."

The three of us stood by and watched–me in wonder, the rest with expecting but knowing expressions–as Isis cupped the two halves of the cloudy stone in her hands. She closed her eyes while a soft hum radiated out from where she stood, filled the air with a calm vibration. Crisp white light grew in her cinched hands, spilling out from the cracks until it was too hard to look at.

I pinched my eyes shut as I turned away, shielding my face from the warming light until I felt it flee the room and the slight chill of room temperature take its place. I blinked away the film and looked to find her standing there with the stone perfectly intact. She held it out for Silas.

He accepted it cautiously and slipped it in his pocket. "Thank you."

"So, how do we plan to find Horus' soul in a sea of thousands?" I asked Anubis.

He stared at me for a moment, seemingly willing me to recall my brief time down in the Underworld and how he'd pulled me from the river. I remembered then, how the arm that touched the water to yank me out had been singed with death. Yeah, it took no time to heal, but it also took even less time for it to eat away at his flesh.

A second of worry flashed in his beady eyes. "Leave that part to me. But it's best we go tonight. There's something I have to do first."

***

Silas and I dragged our tired feet across the colony and back to my quarters as we waited for Anubis to do…whatever it is he insisted he had to do. I tried to think of what it could be, with our window of time so limited. It must have been important.

I shut the door behind us and clicked the lock with a sigh. My body vibrated with a mix of adrenaline and exhaustion. My emotions had been on a never-ending roller coaster since my arrival here, and there was only so much more I could take.

My hands nervously braided together in front of me. "So, you're *absolutely* sure you want to do this?"

Silas stood in the middle of the generous space I lived in. "Andie, I assure you, even though you may question it, you come first. If it's ever a choice between you and my brother, I'll always choose you no matter how I may feel about it. That's a commitment I made not just to you, but to myself."

I chewed at my lip. "No, I never want to be that person. The ultimatum girl."

I thought back then, to the moment my hand slipped over Horus' arm in the temple. He was going to stop. I could feel it. The look on his face when the cube finished opening on its own…It was instant regret.

There might just be hope for the guy yet.

I managed a smile. "Let's not talk about that right now. I don't want to spend these few moments we have drenched in worry and what ifs."

He plunked down on the edge of the bed and leaned forward on his lap. "What do you propose we talk about, then?"

"Oh, I dunno. How about this fancy new stone I have in my pocket?" I swayed over to him, let my leg brush against his, and he fixed his hand around my thigh. "We haven't really had the chance to discuss it. What it really means. Like, how you're stuck with me for eternity now. Has it sunk in yet?"

Silas tipped his head back and peered up at me with a longing in his eyes. "It sunk in for me long before the stone was ever made. Andie, I can't live without you. After this is all over, when we put my brother back in his stone and stop Set from destroying the world, we can leave this place knowing it's finally safe for the Star People. Knowing that humanity will evolve the way they were always meant to."

His fingers trailed up my inner thigh, and I combed my hands through his soft hair. "And where would we go?" I asked him softly.

Silas' shoulders rolled. "Anywhere you want. We could claim a small island in the middle of nowhere and live in peace. We could stay here and help the Star People find proper homes. Liberate the cities, help them all join peacefully. Or we could…go back."

My pulse tightened. "Back? You mean…"

"Yes, if you wanted. If we are successful, then my purpose of returning to the past is done. It's why I had planned on coming back to you, anyway. To the future."

"B-but we destroyed the keystone."

He tapped his forehead with a grin. "I make another one."

A new sense of hope flourished in my as I considered

the possibility. Go home. Where it's safe and comfortable. But would it be? Would the actions we've taken here in the past change the future I came from for the better or worse?

I shook the thoughts from my mind and smiled down at him as I wrapped my arms around his neck. "Let's not worry about any of that right now. One thing at a time. And, since we're stuck waiting for your cousin, we finally have a moment to stop and breathe." I leaned down and kissed his soft, wide lips but couldn't stop the giddy grin that appeared there. "To celebrate the fact that you practically married me this week."

Silas reeled back mockingly. "Oh, is that so? Married? That's a bit of a leap."

I pinched his chin playfully and pulled his face back to mine. "You gave me part of your soul to create a stone that would make me immortal. If that's not some kinda commitment, then I don't know what is."

He chuckled lightly and both his hands gripped the back of my thighs, hauling me closer into his embrace. His lips were on my neck, his words a whisper against my skin between kisses. "So how would you like to celebrate, Mrs. Kalem?"

I leaned into him and we fell backward onto the bed where I wrapped a leg over his waist. Our bodies moulded together, moving in waves of warmth and desire. My lips moved against his. can think of one way.

CHAPTER TWENTY

For someone who's apparently alive, I've sure spent my fair share of time in the Underworld. The deep, hollow echo of the dark cave system enwrapped me in an uncomfortable blanket of unease. I hated it down here. It reeked of death and sadness.

I stood with Silas near the edge of the river, its eerie green glow illuminating the slick black stone around us. To the trained ear, the faintest cries and moans of the dead could be heard in the rushing waters. That was me. I'd been down there, letting the current take me away. And how willing I was. A chill ran through me and I shivered it off.

I looked at a nervous Anubis. "Thank you."

His brow cinched together at the base of his long snout.

"For what?"

I hugged myself tightly. "For saving me that night. For pulling me from the river and putting me back in my body."

A pause held the chilly space between us.

"As far as I saw it, you were my only chance at getting Amun back."

I felt my cheeks fill with an embarrassing heat. "Oh, yeah, that's right." I looked away and Silas' hand rubbed my back. I felt foolish for assuming Anubis did it because he cared about me. I was a stranger to him that night.

Anubis let out a puff of air. "But I also knew that if Amun trusted you with his amulet, then you were important to him and, eventually, would become important to me, too."

I beamed and relaxed a little, but then remembered. "Your hand that night. It was burned or something."

"Yes," he replied, and one of his arms tensed as he shielded it behind him. "I can't survive the River of Souls, no living thing can. Once I'm in, I'll have limited time to find Horus' soul before the river sucks the life from my body."

"How much time?" Silas asked.

With a look of shame, Anubis moved his arm from behind him to reveal a withered limb. Greyed skin and exposed bone. I could see it healing before my eyes, but it didn't stop the wave of shock that came over me.

He shrugged. "Five minutes, perhaps."

"Jesus!" I shrieked and instinctively reached for his arm but stopped myself. "What did you do?"

"I had to test and see how long I could endure the river."

"My God..." Silas blew out in a whisper. He traded a concerned glance with me.

I stared at Anubis pointedly. "If you're not out in four, then I'm coming in after you."

Silas ripped at my hand. "Like hell you are!" He nodded dutifully to his cousin. "I'll do it."

Anubis slapped his cousin's arm and gripped it firmly. "Well, I'll leave you two to debate my mortality. We've got another clock to worry about." He moved toward the edge of the water and glanced over his shoulder with a worried smile before diving into the river.

We both paced the jagged stone of the bank in silence as we waited. I hauled up my sleeve and turned the face of my hidden watch around. "It's been two minutes. Any sign of him?"

Silas peered down, his eyes scanning the gently moving waters. "No. Not yet."

"He's got less than two more minutes," I told him.

"Anubis said he could endure five."

My eyes widened. "No, five minutes is how long he

could last. If he doesn't appear soon, then we'll be hauling out his dead body."

We continued to pace and another minute passed. I counted down the seconds in my mind. "Ten, nine, eight, seven." Silas tensed and braced himself, ready to dive in. "Six, five, four—"

A shrivelled hand shot up out of the emerald waves and clung to the rocky riverside, causing us to jump back. Eerie steam billowed up from it and Anubis, or what it left of him, dragged himself out. Nothing but exposed bone and ripped flesh hanging from his struggling form.

Silas reached for him, but Anubis' gurgled voice echoed through the cavern. "No! I'm covered in it. Don't touch me."

We had no choice but to stand there and watch painfully as he fought tirelessly to extract himself from the River of Souls. His one arm still in the water, the last to come out, and I realized why. It pulled along a soul. Ghostly boned fingers reached out to claw it back in with them, but Anubis wretched it with one last haul and he collapsed on the ground with the glowing figure next to him.

My mouth gaped at the gruesome scene before me. Unable to fathom my next move. Or even my next word. I could already see the immortal power that lived within Anubis, working to heal his emaciated body. Filling in the holes of raw flesh, repairing the deteriorating bones. Even so, it didn't lessen the urge to gag at the sight of it. Of his pain, the sacrifice he'd made for the love of his cousin. Or perhaps he had his own reasons for wanting to save Horus.

"Where the hell am I?" a musical voice sounded off the walls. Horus' soul wavered in place, unanchored to the world, as he peered around with infant eyes. "What's happening?"

"You don't remember what Set did?" Silas asked him.

He struggled through the confusion that plagued his see-through face. "Set. Yes." He nodded slowly, remembering. Then anger filled his expression, and he outstretched his floating arms to examine them. "How could he do this to me?"

"How could *he* do this to *you*?" I gawked. "How could *you* do this to *us*? To the world?"

"I had a plan," he snapped. "I was going to defeat Set and save your precious world, and everyone would have loved me for it."

Silas hissed a sigh. "You're nothing but a jealous brat."

Anubis still lay on the ground, recovering, and we let him do it in peace as we chastised Horus.

I narrowed my eyes at his glowing form, trying not to imagine myself in such a state. "That was a stupid idea. No one is strong enough to defeat Set."

His chin quivered slightly as he raised it defiantly. "I also had a back-up plan."

Silas flew into an enraged lecture with his brother as I took a step back, immersing myself in thought. I pooled together all the events of the last few days, mixed them with all my hunches, and searched for the holes. This is what I knew. Only an Elder God can defeat another Elder God, but Isis is the only one we had, and she's weakened without her counterpart to draw power from. Osiris. Then I recalled what Set muttered in the temple before he crushed the life from Horus.

Our secret dies with you.

Suddenly, a stark chill ran through me, carrying with it the sting of realization. It felt like a betrayal, but it was so much more than that. I tightened my stare at Horus and shoved at Silas' shoulder as I pushed myself to the center of their argument.

"Why would Set kill you so swiftly and ensure you'd never return?" My words cut through the air and Horus let his nervousness rise to the surface. "He said that the secret dies with you."

Silas reached out to grab his brother but stopped himself. It would do no good. He had no physical form to grab. "What. Secret?"

Horus stood silently, almost ashamed, but masked it with defiance.

Silas turned to me. "What is it? What are you getting at?"

Horus sighed in defeat. "Because I helped him do it."

My hand flinched to my face and covered a gasp that squeezed from my mouth. "Jesus…"

Anubis couldn't hold on. He plopped down on a large rock and braced himself with hands on his knees. What must be going through his mind, I wondered? His cousin and his own father worked together to kill and hide the body of the only man who loved him like a son. And he just helped save one of them. How conflicted he must feel.

"Listen here," Silas pushed through his teeth. "This is what's going to happen. We'll put you back in your amulet on one condition. You tell us exactly where to find Osiris."

The wretched trickster searched our faces, peering into our wide and angered eyes as if looking for something. Then, when his transparent face plumped with a sly idea, I knew he caught on to our plan to keep him in the stone.

"I'll agree, only if you swear to put me back in my body afterward."

Silas all but jumped out of his own skin. "And let you continue to ruin our lives and the future of humanity?" A guffaw chopped from his mouth. "I think not."

Horus folded his arms smugly. "No deal then."

Before Silas could toss his brother's soul back in the river, I hauled at his sleeve and dragged him aside.

"Look," I said, my voice lowered. "Maybe we should do it."

I never let my stare waver from the undeserving soul before me and mulled my lips together as I crossed my arms tightly. The longer I let the idea sit in my mind, the more it made sense. Horus dared meet my gaze, and I flashed him a look that could kill.

"You know where Osiris is, don't you?"

"What?" Silas' shocked tone matched Anubis' from the floor. Hastily, he yanked the milky amulet from his pocket and dangled it in front of his brother. "Tell us the truth or you'll never see this again. I'll toss you back in the damn river myself."

Anubis struggled to his feet and, much like a dog, shook the remnant of enchanted water from his skin and fur. He stalked clumsily over to us.

Horus rolled his eyes. "Fine. Yes, I know where parts of our father are hidden."

Silas spun around and stomped over to a loose patch of gravel and kicked at it with a roar of frustration. Horus and I exchanged an odd look, one that almost felt laced with regret, and I weighed back, confused. Why was he so defensive with his brother, but let me see these slight glimpses of his apparent diffidence? His expression hardened when Silas stalked back to us.

He jabbed a finger at his brother. "How do you know where our father is? And I want the truth. *How* do you know where Set hid parts of our father's body?"

once more.

"Are you okay to walk?" he asked Anubis as he stuffed the rock back in his pocket.

Anubis pushed to his feet. Most of his flesh had filled in, but his usual jet-black skin still paled with the ashy grey of death. But he nodded. "Yes. I can make it back."

"Good." Silas turned toward the exit. "We should get out of here now."

We both followed him up and out of the deep cave system of the Underworld entrance and emerged to the world above. I sucked in a fresh breath of air, let it fill my lungs and wash away what little it could. But the outside world didn't look as it did just a short while ago, when we'd last left it.

"Oh my god…" I whispered with a rush of tears that tickled my eyes. Disbelief held me in place.

I scanned the horizon over the vast landscape that was once alive with dunes and oases. With a city and small villages full of people. Mountains of sand covered every inch as far as the eye could see. The Great Pyramids in the distance were half swallowed by the work of Set. The faint hint of rooftops smattered in the dunes below.

"The entire city is…gone," Silas spoke with strain.

I shook my head and failed to contain the tears that spilled out over. "All those people." The three of us turned and shared in the sorrow, chests heaving with the

"But I made a promise to you."

I shrugged. "I just–I don't see another way at this point. We're running out of time. Set is unleashing chaos on the city and soon all of Egypt. And who knows what he'll be able to do once he finds his actually body." He still didn't seem convinced. I took his hand in mine, willed him to calm. "We can put those gold cuffs on his body before we resurrect him."

I could see him fighting with the logic, his face twisted every which way. This was killing him. The pull between his heart and his mind, between duty and life. I bounced back and forth on my heels as I waited for him to come to the only obvious choice we had to pick.

"Fine." He stormed over to where his brother hovered next to Anubis. "You get your way. Again. We'll put you in this stone and resurrect your body, with the promise that you'll tell us how and where to find our father."

"Deal," Horus replied, self-satisfied. He practically hummed with brazen superiority.

"Don't make me regret this," Silas said through gritted teeth.

He inhaled a deep sigh filled with regret and glanced between Anubis and I before slowly holding out the quartz that dangled from his fingers. He touched it to his brother's soul and a blinding light flashed. One second Horus was there, the next…his amulet glowed with life flood of emotions. "We're too late. They're all *dead*."

THE END

KINGDOM OF SAND & STARS

Fated Souls

USA TODAY BESTSELLING AUTHOR

CANDACE OSMOND

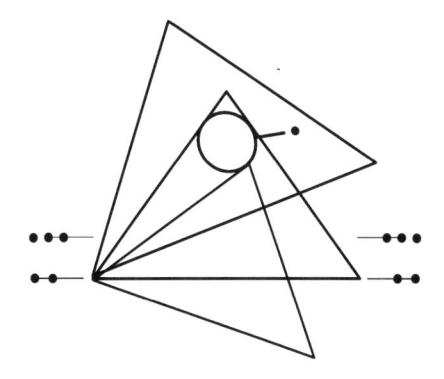

FATED SOULS

Continue Andie's epic story in
this **Sneak Peak** of book three

My heart crashed in its pen the second I stepped foot into the shadowed safety of the colony. I slid against the wall, just inside the narrow overlap of stone, and let my breath harrow in my chest. Silas and Anubis tumbled in behind me and Shadow laid on the floor by my feet while our labored attempts at calming echoed off the looming walls of the Grand Entrance.

We'd escaped the wrath of Set, but just barely.

The city was gone. The once luscious pools of oasis' now buried under heaps of sand as storms that whipped through the air. I managed to lift my gaze to exchange a knowingly glance with my companions, but that was as much as I could muster. My chest burned with exhaustion. Anubis pressed his back against the rough stone, seemingly having a harder time than us. I realized then, as I took a moment to take in the sight of him under the cover of his cloak and yellowed tunic, he'd yet to finish healing from his dip into the Sea of Souls. His usually smooth, dark skin still wreaked of death, slowly healing and coming back together, but his large body lagged with defeat. He needed to rest and heal.

Silas mulled his brother's glowing stone in his hand.

"We should get cleaned up, have some food." I caught his gaze and motioned to Anubis. "Maybe get some rest before we dive into a resurrection spell."

Silas mustered enough composure and stood straight. "Yes, some rest. I know we could all use it."

Anubis tipped his head back and nodded solemnly. "I should pay a visit to Eirik."

"Not a bad idea," I replied. "And, as much as I'd love to collapse in my bed for a hundred years, I should go see my dad first. He'll be worried."

I scooped up Shadow into my arms before we made our way down the large stone staircase, every step my feet took was torturous. But the relief of safety that pushed down kept me together. Set was out there destroying everything in the wake of looking for Isis. But we were alive, we'd made it back. The threat of Horus seemed so laughable now. Juvenile, almost. Especially since we held his fate in our hands.

When we reached the fork in the corridors, Silas patted Anubis on the back. "You be sure to see Eirik. We'll come and check in later."

His cousin left with a tired nod and disappeared down the hallway before we ventured down the other. A comfortable silence carried in the air with us, but I could tell Silas itched to say something. The desire practically hummed around him.

"What's wrong?" I asked, my voice hoarse.

He waited a beat. "What do you mean?"

"I can tell you want to say something," I told him. "Just by the way you're breathing." I stole a sideways glance at him, and the corner of his mouth twitched.

"You're strange."

My shoulders slumped with a quick shrug. "I never claimed to be otherwise."

We turned a corner and a sleeping Shadow stirred in my arms. I held him tighter.

"I'm just worried," Silas admitted.

"About what?"

He shrugged and shook his head helplessly. "Everything. I mean, what is there not to worry about? My uncle will burn this planet to the ground in his search for my mother. And I nearly lost my brother today, indefinitely.

I–" Silas pursed his lips as he thought. "I didn't know how I truly felt about that until it became a reality. We'd spent millennia arguing and fighting over the right to exist. But now I see it for what it truly was. Just sibling rivalry."

A coarse guffaw escaped my chest. "I could argue otherwise."

Silas came to a halt and spun around to face me. "What my brother did to you will not go unpunished." His tense expression melted away as his fingertips brushed my cheek. "He'll never lay a hand on you again. I swear it."

My hand cupped his over my shoulder and I tried to smile for him, but I just couldn't. Wetness filmed my eyes and immediately matched in his. "And what about what he's done to you? The endless jealousy, the inability to let you be happy, framing you for murder." When Silas let his gaze fall, I squeezed his hand tighter until our stares locked once again. "For trapping in your amulet for over a thousand years."

"When you can live forever, a few thousand years means nothing," he said warmly. A futile attempt to assure me he was fine with it all.

I shook my head and let his hand fall from my arm. "Still doesn't make it right."

Silas peered down at the pulsating stone in his grasp and weighed it in his palm with a distant expression. "Let's just deal with the issue at hand. We'll decide what fate my brother deserves when the time comes."

"One thing at a time." My mouth widened, a smile that couldn't reach my eyes even if I wanted it to.

Silas gave a single nod and repeated with a sigh. "One thing at a time."

We continued together toward the heart of the colony, the Great Hall. Suppertime was in full swing and the thunder of voices met us in the hallway before we got there. When Silas and I stepped through one of the many archways that opened up to the massive communal space, all eyes immediately shot in our direction and a swarm of colonists came toward us.

Shadow woke in my arms and let out a squeal in response to the cavalcade of noise before leaping to the floor and scurrying off. Voices, too many, laced with fear and anger, bombarded my ears and I flinched back.

"What's happening out there? Are we safe? Should we leave?"

Silas' futile attempt at reining them in only made the crowd more uneased.

With outstretched arms, he tried to speak over the noise. "Calm down, please! Yes, there's danger, but you're all safe down there."

His words didn't even cut through the noise. One man stood on a bench and shouted out over the crowd.

"We need to leave! The God of Chaos and Destruction

is upon us and it's only a matter of time before he finds the colony."

Another man engaged. "And where would we go? We could be walking right into his hands and risking the lives of everyone down here. To those who choose to stay."

"Then we make them all go!"

"As if the threat of Horus wasn't enough. When will it end?!"

Silas turned and peered back over his shoulder to where I stood. His expression pleaded for me to tell him what to do. But I had no idea. They weren't wrong in their concerns. Set was tearing up the whole world above in search of the goddess, and she was down here with everyone. Amongst the Star People. If Set found a way to track her or discovered the existence of the sanctuary, we'd all be sitting ducks.

I took a step toward him and whispered in his ear. "Just assure them. Promise that we're taking care of it."

He sucked in a deep breath and grabbed a chair before hopping upon it. "Please! Stay calm." The noise level lessened as they all turned their attention to him. "Look, I know you're all scared. I know you've been hearing the whispers of what's happening on the surface. And you're right. Set has been freed." Panicked whispers rose. "But I swear, you're all safe down here. The colony provides cover that you simply cannot get above. There's…nothing left up there. It's all buried under the sand."

The widened stares and resounding gasps twisted in my stomach and I had to look away.

A Venuvian stepped forward, their eyes glistening with worry. "You mean…all those people…"

Silas nodded solemnly. "Yes. There could be survivors but," he looked to me and pursed his lips, "it's not likely. The city is gone. The outer villages…there's no sign of them up there. Everything's under a mass of sand. If the entrance to the colony weren't so high up the mountain, we'd never had gotten back in."

Unease shifted through the crowd as they spoke amongst themselves. Silas cleared his throat, demanding their attention. I stared up at him admiringly, surprised at how easily he commanded a group of people such as this. As if he were meant to rule. Destined to govern over them. He once told me his family weren't gods, were never meant to be worshipped. That may be partially true, but there was no doubt in my mind that the man I loved was meant for something greater.

I don't know what urged me, but I grabbed my own chair and elevated myself to stand next to him. Silas regarded me with surprise, and I smiled as my fingers slipped into his. I'm here, I'll always be here. And, just like the strange otherworldly tether that had always tugged us together, he nodded in understanding. As if he could… feel my thoughts.

I turned to the mass of people. "Listen up! I know you're scared and unsure. I am, too. We all are. But I swear, we have a plan to stop Set. We're working on it. You just have to trust us."

Find out what happens next in book three of **Kingdom of Sand & Stars**, **Fated Souls**!

"A Time Travel Series to Give Outlander a Run for its Money!"

⭐⭐⭐⭐⭐ - *InDTale Magazine*

And if you love the **high stakes danger**, **magic**, and **epic fated romance** of **Kingdom of Sand & Stars** then you'll devour Candace's other **Time Travel Fantasy Series Dark Tides**. Can Dianna charm the crew of **The Devil's Heart** before they kill her ancestors, or will she just fall deeper under the captain's spell?

ABOUT THE AUTHOR

Candace Osmond is a **#1 International** &
USA TODAY Bestselling Author of Fantasy Romance.
She's also an Award-Winning Screenwriter.
She currently resides on the rocky East Coast of
Canada with her husband, two kids, and bulldog.

Connect with Candace online! She **LOVES** to hear
from readers!

AuthorCandaceOsmond.com

Check out all of Candace's book merch and signed
paperbacks in her reader merch shoppe,
Death by Reading!

Manufactured by Amazon.ca
Bolton, ON